A NOVEL BASED ON THE LIFE OF

JUDGE JOHN J. SIRICA

NO PERSON
ABOVE THE LAW

Cynthia Cooper

Barbera Foundation, Inc.
P.O. Box 1019
Temple City, CA 91780

Copyright © 2018 Barbera Foundation, Inc.
Cover photo: Danita Delimont / Alamy Stock Photo
Cover design: Suzanne Turpin

More information at www.mentorisproject.org

ISBN: 978-1-947431-21-8

Library of Congress Control Number: 2018964451

The Mentoris Project is a series of novels and biographies about the lives of great men and women who have changed history through their contributions as scientists, inventors, explorers, thinkers, and creators. The Barbera Foundation sponsors this series in the hope that, like a mentor, each book will inspire the reader to discover how she or he can make a positive contribution to society.

Contents

Foreword

First and foremost, Mentor was a person. We tend to think of the word *mentor* as a noun (a mentor) or a verb (to mentor), but there is a very human dimension embedded in the term. Mentor appears in Homer's *Odyssey* as the old friend entrusted to care for Odysseus's household and his son Telemachus during the Trojan War. When years pass and Telemachus sets out to search for his missing father, the goddess Athena assumes the form of Mentor to accompany him. The human being welcomes a human form for counsel. From its very origins, becoming a mentor is a transcendent act; it carries with it something of the holy.

The Mentoris Project sets out on an Athena-like mission: We hope the books that form this series will be an inspiration to all those who are seekers, to those of the twenty-first century who are on their own odysseys, trying to find enduring principles that will guide them to a spiritual home. The stories that comprise the series are all deeply human. These books dramatize the lives of great men and women whose stories bridge the ancient and the modern, taking many forms, just as Athena did, but always holding up a light for those living today.

Whether in novel form or traditional biography, these books plumb the individual characters of our heroes' journeys.

The power of storytelling has always been to envelop the reader in a vivid and continuous dream, and to forge a link with the subject. Our goal is for that link to guide the reader home with a new inspiration.

What is a mentor? A guide, a moral compass, an inspiration. A friend who points you toward true north. We hope that the Mentoris Project will become that friend, and it will help us all transcend our daily lives with something that can only be called holy.

—Robert J. Barbera, President, Barbera Foundation
—Ken LaZebnik, Founding Editor, The Mentoris Project

Prologue

Standing with his back to the door of the chambers, John loops his right arm into the wide sleeve of the black robe, slipping the whole of it around his blazer and trousers, and taking his time fixing the hooks on one side of the opening into the eyes on the other side. The tradition of the black robe, dating back centuries, appeals to him as much as his title: Judge John Joseph Sirica. The designation hasn't worn thin for him in the sixteen years since he came to the bench. And now, in 1973, he can claim one more word, added two-and-a-half years ago: *Chief* Judge for the District of Columbia, Federal District Court.

"Judge!" Todd calls from a doorway outside the chambers, where he is peeking into the courtroom.

His law clerk, Todd Christofferson, is a tall fellow, well over six feet, compared to John's taut five feet, six inches. They look quite a pair when they stride through the hallways of the courthouse.

"There's a massive crowd out there." Todd angles his hand over his mouth to muffle his words.

The judge nods. Of course. He'd expected as much—that's why he moved the trial to the big Ceremonial Courtroom on the sixth floor. This is, undoubtedly, a better facility to try the cases of the seven defendants arrested for burglarizing the Democratic Presidential Campaign Headquarters in the Watergate office complex. This courtroom is more spacious, more commanding than his own courtroom on the second floor. Inside the Ceremonial Courtroom a wall of marble cladding behind the judge's bench endows a sense of import with nearly life-size figurines of Hammurabi, Moses, Solon, and Justinian, personages from the law's history. As many as 350 people can be seated in the eight elongated rows of benches, and the press, especially the *Washington Post*, has been increasingly paying attention. Outside the front doors of the courtroom are banks of telephone booths of the sort preferred by newspaper reporters.

The judge slides over to the doorway to take a look inside the courtroom. He can't help himself. In front are his bailiff, his courtroom clerk, and the court reporter. At the defendants' table sit the accused burglars and their lawyers. Lots of lawyers. On the prosecutors' side are three men from the Justice Department District of Columbia Criminal Division, which handles major cases from Washington, D.C. Behind them, in the banks of seats for spectators, are reporters, observers, even sketch artists who snatched front-row seats and now sit poised with graphite pencils and oversize pads, ready to capture the moment. They always draw the judge with his thick hair combed back smoothly from his face, black with tinges of silver and gray, bushy eyebrows, bags under his eyes, and deep craggy lines framing his mouth.

Not bad for sixty-eight years of age, he thinks. Still at his fighting weight.

The judge closes the door to the courtroom. "I have a hunch that we're going to find out there's more to this Watergate event than meets the eye," he says, tightening his tie knot.

"I'll do my best to keep up," says Todd. He's only been on the job a few months. Ever since his boss, Judge Sirica, decided to take on this case himself rather than assign it to one of the fourteen other judges, Todd has been digging heavily into criminal procedure. He sits in the library on the third floor at every opportunity, trying to be ready for any question that comes up in court. Sure, the postponement from November '72 to January '73 gave him an extra buffer, but the cause of the delay— the pinched nerve that's made it hard for the judge to sit for extended periods—is a daily worry.

"Is the gavel on the bench?" the judge asks.

"Yes, sir."

"Then tell the bailiff to call order and we'll see where this takes us," says the judge, turning back inside. "Ya know me: 'Let the chips . . .'"

"'. . . fall where they may,'" they finish in unison.

The fascinating part of being a judge is that every day is different. Before becoming a judge, Sirica was a prosecutor and a criminal defense attorney and a civil trial lawyer, and even counsel on a Congressional committee investigating nefarious dealings. Sometimes, he realizes, it's tempting to think he's seen it all— gamblers, murderers, petty thieves, extortionists, monopolists, con artists, wheelers-and-dealers, schemers of every variety.

But this—he's never seen a case like this before.

Five men in suits caught cold in the middle of the night

planting eavesdropping devices in the headquarters of a major political party and photographing documents from their files. Another two accused of making the arrangements. At a glance, it could look like a petty break-in, and that's how half the town has treated it for months since the first arrests on June 17, 1972.

Having watched the way the powerful act in D.C., the judge is asking questions, if only of himself. Who would have an interest in wiretapping a political party, unless it were the other major political party? Doesn't this look more like political espionage than five or seven guys out on a lark, as some are claiming? The people working for President Richard M. Nixon dub it a "third-rate" burglary, and in November, just a couple of months ago, the president was re-elected by one of the largest margins in history.

The people at the head of government have been trying to push this matter aside. But the facts are peculiar, to say the least. Some of the burglars have backgrounds in the FBI and the CIA. The men with the tools are from Florida and were involved in Cuban anti-Castro operations. They have fancy equipment. These are not local guys from the pool hall acting on a whim. When arrested, they give false names and have fake identification. The *Washington Post* writes that large sums of money are being exchanged.

Something fishy is going on, but exactly what is not clear.

The judge reaches for a legal pad on the desk.

Who told these men to do this?

He scribbles and underlines it three times.

Who paid? Who is responsible? Why were they there?

4

These are the questions that keep coming back to him. Not what happened or how it happened or how the arrests were made so much as who and why.

He's decided to sit as the judge on this case himself because, as a Republican, he might have an advantage. If things get sticky for the defendants, a Democrat might be accused of partisanship. With his conservative roots, he can't be accused of putting party above justice. He and President Nixon agree on many things, and law and order is one of them.

Todd steps back in and taps on the inner door.

"Everyone's ready. The jury is prepared to enter," he whispers.

The judge waves Todd on. He needs one more minute. He smoothes out the wrinkles on his pants and checks each of the hooks on his robe from chest to belt. Then he steadies his eyes on the stripes on the flag behind the desk, lets his lower legs grip the floor, and tightens his fingers into a fist. He closes his eyes.

More than forty years in the law—it seems that his entire life, every scrappy encounter, every modest success and burly failure, has brought him to this one place. It is, he thinks, a moment in time. He opens his eyes, stretches his fingers.

Let the chips fall where they may. He's ready for whatever lies ahead.

Part One

JOHNNY SIRICA FIGHTS HIS WAY INTO THE LAW

Chapter One

A HARDSCRABBLE LIFE

With the final school bell of the year, Johnny nearly floats down the street. He's aiming for the shop where men come to see the barber—that's his father, Ferdinando Sirica. If he sweeps the floor really well, it might alleviate his father's coughing—and if any customers come in, Johnny can pick up some good stories. To be sure, there aren't many customers. Even at seven years of age, Johnny knows the cash register isn't ringing enough to keep them afloat.

"Put up yer dukes!" Andy races from behind and taps Johnny on the side of the head.

Johnny swings around quickly, left fist high, right fist pulled back, ready to strike.

"You're dead meat to me!" he says. He lets his right fist thump into his younger brother's chest, being careful not to knock him down.

"Not so hard. I'm only playing." Andy grabs his chest and blinks his eyes to keep back tears.

"Then don't come up from behind," Johnny says, putting his arm around Andy's shoulder.

His brother is as tall as Johnny is, even if he's a year and a half younger. They've been watching the amateur boxers who fill the clubs in town—Johnny sometimes sneaks into a corner of the room with his older cousin, Fonsy.

"Okay, then, let's practice-hit," says Andy. "Count of three. One, two—"

While Andy holds his ground, Johnny races down the street.

"You can't catch me!" Johnny yells over his shoulder. He's not faster than his brother, and not even very athletic, but he's got a good head start and it's a path he knows well.

Lots of Siricas live in Waterbury, Connecticut. Johnny's father, Ferdinando, first arrived as a seven-year-old child from San Valentino Torio, Italy, near Naples, with his father, Joseph, and stepmother, Margaret. Immediately after their boat docked at the Emigrant Landing Depot of New York City in 1887, they headed eighty miles north to the small city on the Naugatuck River.

Streams of other Italian immigrants seeking better opportunities made the same trek as the word spread about Waterbury, a fast-growing industrial center. In 1880, Waterbury's population was 17,000; by 1910, it's grown to 73,000, mostly immigrants. They fill jobs in the brass mills that earn Waterbury the moniker of "Brass Center of America," or find their way to the clock and watch factories that stretch across the town.

Not far away, New Haven is also a magnet for Italians. That's where Ferdinando—everyone calls him Fred—met Rose Zinno, whose parents, Nicholas and Antoinette, were from Naples. Fred convinced her to join him in Waterbury, and by the time Fred was twenty-four, baby John was on the way.

Fred wasn't much of a factory man. "Rather run my own life," he'd say. He learned barbering by hanging around a shop in Waterbury as a child, lathering and cleaning up. But as an adult, he found the barber trade didn't offer much to pay the rent. To make ends meet, Rose took a job in a grocery store and they rented a single-room apartment behind it. Even Johnny saw that his father needed a bigger base of customers to push his income past $16 a week. More money and better air to keep Fred's cough at bay; the doctor has taken to calling it "tubercular."

Midsummer in 1911, Rose shakes the headboard on the bed that Johnny and Andy share.

"You need to get dressed," she says. "Your father's doctor says he can't live by the factories anymore. He needs someplace warmer."

The two boys and their parents trundle to the train station in the dark to catch the morning line headed to Florida. In Atlanta, Fred meets a man who tells him about a business prospect in Ohio. Just as suddenly, they are headed for Dayton. It's the first of a half-dozen times that the same scenario plays out, as they move from town to town, state to state—Ohio, then Florida, Louisiana, Virginia, and then back to Florida again.

By 1918, the small Sirica family lands in Washington D.C., renting a two-room apartment above a shoe shop at 11th and O.

Wherever they live, Johnny gets busy, trying to make a little money to help the family out. He sells ice cream on the beach or newspapers on the streets or takes other odd jobs. School is hopeless—with the constant moves, he's missed months and years of grade school. Anyhow, he's thinking in a different direction. Now that he's fourteen and in D.C., Johnny has a career plan. He wants to become an auto mechanic, and lands a job as a grease monkey at Gish's Garage at 17th and U Street.

One of Johnny's main assignments requires him to squeeze beneath the cars and dump out the grit in the oil filters. He has packed on a few pounds and this task isn't very easy with the heft he carries. Worse, it's boring being under a car all day. He takes a few shortcuts—wiping around the filters instead of emptying them out.

"John, come here! Now!" Mr. Gish screams across the buzz of equipment in the garage. "This customer is complaining his car don't run right, John! So I get under there and look what I find." He shows John a pan filled with dirty oil and grit. "How'd that happen, John?"

The customer, standing by the car, politely looks away.

"I—I—I . . ." Johnny stammers. He brushes his eye with the back of his hand.

"You what?"

"I guess I didn't do it the way you showed me, Mr. Gish."

"You didn't do it, period! Longtime customer, this man. Good customer. Decent man. And this is how you treat him?"

"I'm sorry, sir." Johnny folds his rags and puts them on a shelf. "You don't have to pay me, Mr. Gish."

At home, Johnny rushes into the bathroom. His stomach turns in knots, and when he looks in the mirror, he wants to throw up. He bangs his palm on the edge of the sink.

"Never," he whispers to himself. Never again does he want to feel that he can't look himself in the mirror.

At dinner, his father bellows when he hears that Johnny is no longer at Gish's.

"This is a problem, John! You need school! You got to get an education."

"I'm not good at it."

"Your mother's found a place that will take you. An academy called—"

"Emerson," Rose cuts in from across the kitchen table. "You can go at night."

"And do a job in the day," says Fred.

"I don't see why. You never—"

"If I ever find you working as a barber, I'm going to break your arm!" Fred points his finger in Johnny's face. "Ya hear me? I will BREAK your arm."

Johnny begins at Emerson and gets a job hawking newspapers.

One good thing about the Capital City is that the people have a seemingly insatiable desire for news. Every day. Several times a day. Johnny shouts out headlines for the *Evening Star* and the *Washington Post*, and with each "EXTRA! EXTRA!" he learns more about this town. Two things seem to be on people's minds in the District of Columbia: politics and sports.

Stories about the "Manassa Mauler," Jack Dempsey, fill the papers. He's punching his way to becoming the World Heavyweight Boxing Champion, and when he does on July 4, 1919, it's top of the news the next morning, and not just on the sports pages. John screams out the headlines: "EXTRA EXTRA! Manassa Mauler Jack Dempsey Defeats Jess Willard for Title!" "Dempsey Is Winner in 3 Vicious Rounds!" "Dempsey Is a Real Champion Who Will Last." Johnny even buys a paper for himself and shows his brother.

"Dempsey has a baby face, but you can't let it trick you," Johnny explains to Andy. "He gets in there and punches and punches. Never still for an instant. Hands in motion at all times. He knocks Willard down seven times in the first round. Never been done. Everyone thought it was over—Dempsey's leaving the arena when the ref says the bell rang before the final count and calls Dempsey back to the ring. Two more rounds. 'Amazing speed and two murderous hands. The best left hook of all times'—that's what the announcer says. Willard never gets up for the fourth round. His manager throws in the towel." Johnny waves his hand over the picture in the *Washington Post*. "In one hundred and ten degrees. Before tens of thousands of people. In Toledo, Ohio. Listen to this one. Someone put it in a letter: 'A hundred thousand jostled one another and stared transfixed at the new fabulous being: DEMPSEY!'"

Johnny puts the paper down and imitates the expression in the picture—a rugged toughness tempered by a charming, wry expression that could be mistaken for a smile.

"Dempsey! A right, a left, a right, a right. And then *bam*—left hook! Of course he's a few inches taller than me," Johnny says.

Andy laughs. "Half a foot taller! But he probably weighs the same!"

Johnny punches the air. He can't deny that his appetite is beyond healthy. Who can turn down his mother's spaghetti, her lasagna, her sausages? Or the Southern grits with eggs on top and a few extra spices, the way she learned to make them in Florida and Louisiana, but with a Neapolitan twist? And the homemade cherries soaked in wine on special occasions. Still, he's now carrying 185 pounds, and at his height, he's more beanbag shape than he is boxing material.

"I can still whup you," Johnny says to Andy. "Ya wanna see?"

Andy snorts and walks away.

The Washington news is also loaded with politics. There's always some committee or some appointment or some vote.

Prohibition and suffrage and President Wilson and German war reparations fill the papers, and then there's the election for president in 1920 when Warren Harding wins the White House. Johnny moves to selling papers at an actual newsstand at Pennsylvania and 11th Street NW, right in front of the *Washington Star* building. The stand has out-of-town newspapers, foreign newspapers, racing forms—all kinds of material to read and absorb.

Johnny is still calling out the headlines there when *The Wall Street Journal* reports on April 14, 1922, that Albert Fall, the Secretary of the Interior under President Harding, has given a lease to a government-owned oil platform at Teapot Dome, Wyoming, to an oil-company friend in secret. The senator from Wyoming announces an investigation and especially wants to know about a sudden upgrade in Secretary Fall's lifestyle.

At home, Johnny spins out details during dinner. "They're saying there might be bribery involved. At the highest levels of the government! In the president's cabinet."

He has an air of authority that makes Andy stop eating.

"How come you know so much?" Andy asks.

Before Johnny can answer, Fred knocks his knuckles on the table. "Imagine someone trusted with a position such as that and using it to line his own pockets. That's not right, is it, Rose?"

She nods. "The number of times people lied to you, Fred, telling you a business is good, but then there's always something wrong with it. It's a rotten shame."

"Crooks! They're a bunch of crooks! Honesty and integrity," Fred points first to one son and then to the other. "You deal with people right. You hear me? That's what justice is about."

Chapter Two

A ROCKY ROAD

Union Station is bustling when Johnny goes to meet his cousin Fonsy in September 1922. Fonsy has come to D.C. from Waterbury, where his father is a barber like Johnny's father. For years, the older cousin has been chiding Johnny to be more serious about school, and John finally has some news. After Emerson, he transferred to Columbia Prep, and now he's finished—he has the high school diploma that his father never managed. Fonsy is bound to be impressed.

There's more, too. Now that he's out of high school, he's added another role: working part-time at his father's latest entrepreneurial endeavor. This one is a little pool hall, a bit run-down, but it reminds Johnny of the places in Waterbury where he and Fonsy would sneak in as kids. There are five pool tables and a two-lane bowling alley and a snack bar on the side. It's located on North Capitol near H Street, and above it is the two-room apartment where they live. Andy won't have anything to do with the pool hall, but Johnny helps out, racking up pool balls and playing with the customers, or setting the pins on the bowling alley.

Of course, right after Fred acquires the pool hall, problems begin. A rowdy crowd likes to frequent the place. And then there is the Volstead Act—Prohibition—which seems to be enforced with an extra frenzy in D.C. Agents think nothing of sweeping down on every little establishment, no matter how inconsequential—even a two-lane bowling alley and five-table pool hall. The police activity doesn't dent the activities of the imbibing customers who constantly ask for a squirt of Coca-Cola to guzzle with the whiskey they carry in tonic bottles stashed in their socks.

Johnny sees Fonsy across the wide expanse of the railroad station—he's wearing a jaunty cap with a brim, and has an air of confidence.

"I'm going to law school," Fonsy cuts in even before they reach the exit. "George Washington University Law School. Right here in D.C. People respect lawyers, and I'm going to get some respect for the Siricas. I need you to take me to this address to meet with the registrar." He points to a slip that lists a temporary location, an address on K Street.

"Sure, Fonsy," Johnny says.

At the law school office, Johnny stands in the corner while Fonsy completes the paperwork. Going to law school seems so far away from the days when he trailed behind Fonsy and his older friends to take a dip in the Naugatuck River, or joked with his sister Gertrude while they shared a precious gelato.

The registrar points to Johnny. "You need some papers?" he asks.

"Waiting for my cousin."

"We're looking for smart fellows for a new class. Where'd you go to college?" the man asks.

"I graduated Columbia Prep," Johnny says.

"Columbia Prep? We like that. And then . . . ?"

"I'm only eighteen. I haven't been to college or anything."

"You're in the right place! You don't need a college degree to go to law school in D.C. And we have spaces. Lost a lot of fellows to the war in Europe," the man says. He holds out a sheath of papers.

"Yeah, come on, apply!" Fonsy's eyes are dancing. "We can be buddies in school together. Two Siricas! And you can show me around D.C. What else are you going to do with your life? Sweep up in your father's pool hall?"

John takes the papers from the registrar and fills them out.

When the two go back to the Siricas' apartment, Fred gives Fonsy a bear hug and playfully snatches his hat.

"I hear you're going to be a hotshot," Fred says.

"Yes, sir. Starting law school. George Washington University." Fonsy pauses for dramatic flair. "And this here cousin of mine might be joining me!"

"What's this?" Fred says.

"I only put in an application. I won't know until next week," Johnny says. The idea of being like one of the men who carries a briefcase and buys the *Evening Star* on his way out of a building with soaring pillars gives him a little mental jolt, but he can't manage a smile. "I'm pretty sure they won't take me."

"Rose!" Fred whoops in the direction of the kitchen. "You hear this? Johnny is going to be a bigwig lawyer! Cherries jubilee tonight, all around!"

When Johnny swings over to the registrar's office the next

week, he has already prepared how he'll explain the rejection letter to his father. The registrar hands him a class schedule instead. Johnny reads through the document twice before looking up again.

"You're sure I'm accepted? *John J.* Sirica?" he asks.

"Yes, and you're seated alphabetically, right behind Alphonse Sirica. Make sure you have all your books in advance of the first class."

The schedule is crammed. So many courses, so much Latin. *Prima facie. Res ipsa loquitur. De facto. Stare decisis. Corpus delicti. Dictum. Mens rea. Voir dire. In camera. Sub judice.*

Each case brings up some point of history that simply hadn't made it into Columbia Prep. British common law. Constitutional conventions. Chief Justice John Marshall. When Johnny looks around the class, he sees that most of the students are Fonsy's age and older. They have college degrees; have served in the Great War. They've been abroad. He can yell out the headlines at the newsstand, but standing in front of people and talking— well, the words just don't come. The material swims around in his head, but he isn't able to make heads or tails out of most of it.

"I can't do it," Johnny tells Fonsy as they walk down the school steps during the third week. "Ya know, you'll do fine without me."

The next afternoon, he's in the pool hall, racking balls and brushing the table felt.

"What's going on?" Fred emerges from behind the counter.

"Getting things ready for the night gang." Johnny sweeps his arm across the top of the table without looking up.

"I don't need you to do that. I do that. You're supposed to be reading those fat law books."

"It's not for me. I decided to spend the time at the Y, getting in shape."

"What're you telling me? You dropped out? Is there something wrong in the head with you?"

"Fonsy's been to college. He's good at all those words and that history and whatnot. It's all a confusing jumble to me. I can't make it out." Johnny turns to twist the cue sticks into the holders on the wall, hiding his face from his father. He doesn't want to see the disappointment, and he doesn't want to cry, either. "I'm sorry, Pop. I tried."

John's been going by the YMCA daily now. He's lost thirty pounds already, and he's meeting fellows who wrestle and box and play golf. Stand-up men. They tell him about all sorts of jobs he'd never considered—real estate and hotel management and handling shipping documents for government offices and what it's really like practicing law. After they lift weights together, they walk miles through the city, sometimes ending up at Fred Sirica's pool hall.

"Henry Jawish come looking for you," his father tells him one night when Johnny's setting up pins on the bowling lanes.

"Haven't seen him since we graduated Prep," Johnny says, placing the ten-pin at the corner of the triangle.

"He's going to law school. Like Fonsy! A different one. Georgetown—I think that's the name of it. He thinks maybe you want to look it over since that other place didn't work out."

John recognizes the name Georgetown. It's over on E Street NW between 5th and 6th Streets.

"Maybe," he says.

He and Henry spent every day at Prep together, separated only when Henry went to football practice and Johnny set off for his job at the newsstand. Some people thought they were brothers—"the Jawricas," they called them. Like Johnny, Henry doesn't have a degree beyond Columbia Prep. *If he's going to Georgetown,* Johnny thinks, *maybe I can, too.*

The people at the admissions office don't flinch at the short tenure of his previous law school career, and the 1923 fall semester finds Johnny sitting at Georgetown Law. The law professors here are even meaner than the last bunch—they seem to pride themselves on picking on students. One spots Johnny shrinking behind the man seated in front of him, trying to be invisible, and immediately recognizes a soft target.

"Mr. SEE-reeka," the professor calls, deliberately mispronouncing Johnny's last name.

Johnny stands, as is required, and looks desperately at the casebook on his table for some hidden clue. "It's Sa-RIK-a, sir."

"Do you agree with the analysis in *Marbury v. Madison* that the courts retain the power to declare whether or not a law duly passed by Congress, which sits, after all, as the legally elected representatives of the people, withstands Constitutional muster? Mr. SEE-reeka! I'm not hearing any answers, Mr. SEE-reeka! Is that body of yours attached to a head? Or is that body taking up a space in the classroom because you have no place to go?"

The other students chuckle softly—not so loud as to become the next bull's-eye, but vocal enough for Johnny to hear.

"Mr. SEE-reeka! Do you have a tongue?"

"I'm not sure."

"Not sure of the answer? Not sure of the question? Not sure if you are equipped with all of the components to allow vocalization of your thoughts? Of what are you unsure, Mr. SEE-reeka? Can you please be more specific?"

No one is laughing now. They steadfastly bow toward their writing pads, determined to avoid witnessing the carnage.

Later that day, Johnny pulls Henry aside. "I'm giving you my blank notebooks and fountain pen. I don't see myself sitting here for three years." Johnny shows him a withdrawal slip.

At home, he doesn't say much about dropping out again. His father seems to have troubles of his own. Fred drags himself upstairs to the living quarters and drops his head on the kitchen table.

"Johnny, will you get me a water? Please, son."

He does, and his father takes a light sip. "These people," Fred says, "they don't . . . they don't . . . ."

"Are the agents coming around?"

His father was already hauled in once when the Volstead agents found bootleg alcohol in the men's room. Fred told the police he had nothing to do with it—it must have been the customers. "I play by the rules; don't have any kind of record. I'm an honest businessman," he protested. "These customers don't care. They don't care." The charges were dropped the next day at the arraignment. But after a night in jail, Fred is smoking more than ever.

"No, not agents. Hooligans." He puts the glass down hard on the table and takes three quick puffs from a cigarette before he heads back to work.

Within minutes, Johnny hears yelling and races down to the pool hall. As he turns the corner, he sees a roughneck, Benny German, and two of the other rowdies who follow him around. Benny is reaching over the counter, where Fred is standing.

"We run this place. So you don't be telling us nothin'." Benny grabs at Fred's collar. "We say you stay open late tonight, and ain't no one telling us nothin' different. You get it, ya dirty wop?"

"Hey, Benny German!" The anger gathers in Johnny's throat. "Pick on me if you want to pick on someone."

Benny whirls around. "Whaddya want, you little runt?" He throws a punch right to Johnny's nose.

With split-second timing, Johnny steps six inches to the side and slams Benny on the jaw with a left hook. Benny lands on the floor, flat on his back, out cold. His two pals look at Johnny in surprise, then swoop down and carry Benny out the door. Johnny snaps the lock tight behind them.

Fred collapses in a chair and digs into his pocket for another cigarette—he must be up to smoking three packs a day now, maybe four.

"Rose is right. How did I get into this mess? I got taken again. In New Orleans it was with that no-good restaurant and my no-good, so-called 'partner' running off with the till. Now, some crooks sold me this no-good joint with bad apples in all the barrels. Flat-out robbery, that's what it is." Fred sucks deeply on a cigarette and then coughs hard. "Dishonest, no-good cheats and bums. If I ever hear about you doin' something dishonest, I will take the name 'Sirica' back—you will no longer be my son. You hear me, Johnny? Every cent I had. Robbed."

Two months later, Rose grabs Johnny's arm as he's about to head to the Y. "Your father's decided we're moving. He's sold the place. Or gave it away for whatever pittance he could get out of it. We're going to California."

Just like the old days. The nomadic life from city to city, place to place, state to state. They pack up a four-cylinder Hup-mobile. Rose, Fred, Andy, and John pile in and they head west.

As they slowly make their way across the states, Fred turns his attention to Johnny, as if he's surprised to see him there.

"Why did you drop out? Don't do like me. You got to make something of yourself. Your brother, Andy—I don't have to worry about him. He'll make his way. But you, I don't know what to think. You want to be running from one town to another all your life? Mopping up some joint? Giving a shave and a haircut to other men who don't have a nickel's worth of respect for ya? You should have stayed in the law school like Fonsy. Like that Henry fellow. What's wrong that you don't stick it out? I raised you to be stronger, didn't I? We spent good money getting you a schooling at those prep places. You could be a man who wears a tie. And a watch. And now what? Rose? Rose, do you agree?"

"Yes," his mother says, pretending to look out the window so no one can see the muscles tightening around her mouth. "We wanted something better. We wanted you to do like your cousin. Law school. You belong in law school."

It's easy for them to say, thinks Johnny, *but they didn't have to sit there and be humiliated day after day.* It's over his head; he's tried to tell them. Columbia Prep was good, but not good enough to prepare him for law school.

Finding jobs in Los Angeles turns out to be hard, too. The old story again. Rose tells Johnny one night that they're going to Florida again, where her sister lives.

John writes a letter to Henry:

> *Do me a favor, friend. Will you inquire at the office about the possibility of re-admission? I'll be back in D.C. shortly. This time, I'm going to be stronger."*

Chapter Three

THE ROPES

Georgetown gives him another chance, but it's still grueling. Nine courses in the first year; none are easy. Every time Johnny leaves the classroom, he thinks he'll pack it in. If only it weren't for that image of his mother looking out the car window. *"You belong in law school,"* she'd said. He remembers her voice cracking as if she were holding back a flood of tears.

He keeps going back, day after day. He's not earning any awards, but he's not failing, either.

Weekends, early mornings, and nights, he's at the gym of the Knights of Columbus on 10th Street, near K Street NW. A friend helps him get a job there, and the $100 per month pays for a rooming house on K Street near 14th. The work is enjoyable, too.

Johnny clears his throat one morning to get attention when he comes out of the locker room. "Are we ready?"

He's trying to get better at standing in front of the men. These are lawyers, businessmen, people whose names might be in the *Evening Star* or the *Washington Post*. Most know him as a law student, not a teenager who hasn't even gone to college and whose folks are living on the brink. Still, he's managed to shed the fat around his belly and it takes two hands for the average fellow to reach around his biceps.

The dozen men line up in rows.

"Arms out," Johnny says. "Circle. One, two, three. Reverse. Behind your neck. Stretch your elbows forward. Good. Now knee bends."

After he guides them through the calisthenics, he spars with those who want to test their boxing skills.

He's actually building up a reputation. Small, but feisty. He can throw a punch, and feint when he needs to. Local boxing clubs ask him to join exhibition matches, and he does. The fights are planned for four rounds, and he racks up a couple dozen and even one professional-length ten-rounder. The matches are all in private clubs or smokers rather than in public arenas because of archaic rules that hang over the District. Public boxing matches in the District of Columbia are banned—the same as in many states. They view boxing as unseemly and shady, not an activity to be emulated in "sports." But the number of boxing fans has grown over the years. It's a way for young men to pull them-selves out of poverty—men like Jack Dempsey, whose family lived a rough-and-tumble life in mining country out west. The military starts using boxing to motivate troops, keep them in shape. Dempsey and other boxers become celebrities—stars on radio broadcasts, then in newsreels and film. By the early 1920s, many states are changing their laws to permit legalized boxing. But not D.C.

One of the sparring clients has special sympathy for John-ny's law school travails.

"For goodness' sake, everyone struggles with the first year—that's part of the ritual," Leo A. Rover tells Johnny during a workout session.

Johnny listens intently. Rover is a 1910 Georgetown law grad and assistant U.S. attorney for the District of Columbia.

"You have to tough it out," Rover continues. "That's what got me to where I am."

"I don't know how you did it. I'll scream if there's one more Latin phrase," John says.

"We're going to get you through this, Johnny," Rover says. He tightens the strings on his practice gloves. "What you need to do . . . you need to get to know every single person in your class. You need to build up a group of friends. That's how it works. You say 'Hello' and you say 'Congratulations.' You join groups. You show up. That's the way you get ahead in this town. You got that, Johnny?"

"Yes, sir. I think I understand."

"I can always hire some fellow who knows Latin. What I really need is someone sharp, someone who can read people as much as books. I need attorneys who aren't going to get buffaloed and aren't going to let people pull the wool over their eyes. You get my point here?" Rover begins jabbing at the speed bag.

"Yes, sir. It sounds a lot like boxing."

"Exactly, Johnny. I need people who can be on their toes all the time. Eyes open. You can do that."

In his second and third years of law school, things begin to look up. Johnny moves from all C's to B's, and even an A or two. Between classes, he gets to know the other students—there are seventy-four. They're mostly Catholic like him, even if many come from families who are already well positioned in society. When the last day comes in June 1926, at least he can say he stuck it out. Even if he's not quite in the upper two-thirds. Even if—and he doesn't say this out loud—he never practices law.

The yearbook makes its own assessment: "Johnny has impressed us by his clean-cut manner, his ability to make and keep friends and his avowed determination to master the law. With a large following of friends in every department of the University, he ends his law school career as one of the best-liked men in his class."

But there's another hurdle to becoming a lawyer: passing the bar. Sure, he registered in advance for the bar exam like everyone else in his class, but he's not confident he can pass the three-day test and isn't really sure what he would do in the world of law if he did pass. Rather than sit in the high-pressure examination room, Johnny has a different plan: He will go to Florida where his folks are.

On the morning of the exam, Johnny sits down to breakfast in D.C. to share his farewell plans with Morris Cafritz, a wealthy real estate man he's been training. Normally they meet at six in the morning and drive over to Haines Point for a 3.5-mile jog, and then head over to the Knights of Columbus gym to put on some gloves. Today, they meet at the Ambassador Hotel at 14th and K Street NW; Cafritz is the owner and it's a stone's throw from Johnny's rooming house.

"Leaving?" Cafritz asks when he hears Johnny's intentions. "Not taking the bar? Don't be silly. What do you have to lose by taking it? You might surprise yourself and pass." He pours a second cup of coffee for Johnny.

"Everyone in the class has taken a prep course, but I didn't have the money. You know, I'm counting pennies," Johnny tells him. "Plus, I'm homesick for some decent pasta. Some good old lasagna. Maybe with hand-rolled sausage on the side."

"You'd be a fool and a half not to take the exam. You're going to deep-six the last three years because you're afraid you might fail?"

"That's not what I said." Johnny grabs a piece of toast and slaps jelly on it.

"You didn't *say* that. But it's how you're acting."

"I'm thinking about other options."

"Suppose you want to come back to D.C.?"

"Suppose I don't. I'm turning in all of these today!" Johnny holds up a stack of law books, each one thicker than the next. The law librarian allowed him to borrow them since he was on such a tight budget, but right now, they're feeling heavier than the weights he picks up off the rack in the gym.

"John! Do the right thing. Finish what you started." Cafritz pays the bill and sprints out to a waiting car.

When Johnny heads to Georgetown to return the books, his classmates are lining up for the exam.

"Johnny!" one calls. "He's here, fellas. Our Johnny. We're in luck!"

Before he can count the number of federal circuit courts, he's sitting with a test booklet, struggling over seemingly impossible hypothetical questions.

At the end of the day, the classmates all gather at a local club and review their answers. Johnny shrinks from the conversation. When the last exam session ends, he doesn't wait around. Bar exam results won't be out for months. He's pretty certain what the verdict will be anyhow, and it seems unlikely he'll be back.

∾

In Miami, Johnny and Andy are both making the rounds looking for jobs. John isn't turning up much, trudging through downtown, roaming from one attorney's office to another, offering himself up as a law assistant. At Andy's suggestion, he takes a job driving a jitney to get by. Navigating the streets, he discovers the YMCA. At least he can stay in shape.

John does his usual exercise routine at the Y—jumping ropes, running in place, lifting weights. Then he pounds the six-foot heavy bag with his bare fists to keep his arms in shape.

"Mind if I join you?" A man strapping on boxing gloves also starts hitting the heavy bag. Wordlessly, he points Johnny over to another pair of gloves and the two begin to spar.

Johnny notes that he's about the same height, maybe an inch or two taller, and about his weight, too: 145 pounds. But the fellow must be about twenty years older.

A full hour later, the man puts his arms down, ready to stop.

"You're hard to hit, young man . . . always going away from the punches," he says, pulling off his glove and holding out his hand. "Name's Jack Britton."

"Of course. I know the name," Johnny says.

"You're probably thinking Jack Dempsey," the man says.

"No. Britton. Welterweight champ. First title defeating Ted 'Kid' Lewis in 1916. And then lost to Lewis in 1919. And reclaimed the title on March 17, 1919—knockout in round nine. Held 'til 1922, Madison Square Garden, Mickey Walker—rough loss."

Britton smiles. "You know your stats."

"Used to read up on them at a newsstand in D.C. But I should have known . . . the way you punch—like it's a science and you're dissecting every weak spot."

"'Dissecting'—that's some kind of fancy language for a

boxer. I'm aiming for a little comeback. Need to make up for some real estate losses around here. I guess I wasn't so 'scientific' about that, if you know what I mean. Help me train, and if I win, I'll pay ya ten percent of my earnings."

"You know, that's a lot more traction than I'm getting in the courthouse district."

"That's a messy world," Britton says, unlacing his shoes. "You're good enough to enter some matches and earn some real money. You're little, like me. You're young. You know how to pace yourself. You've got a strong constitution."

Johnny begins going toe-to-toe with Britton every morning. Before long, Britton is back in the ring. When a promoter says he needs another fighter to put on a card at Douglas Stadium, Britton points to Johnny. The opponent: Tommy Thompson, a welterweight at six feet, one inch—seven inches taller than Johnny—and known for having a mean streak. At the weigh-in, he leans over Johnny like he's going to spit on the top of his head.

"You'll be okay," Britton tells him. "He looks tough, but he won't be able to land a punch. Trust your instincts. Get your grounding in the first round. Plant your feet, gather your muscles, focus your mind. Be thinking all the time. He won't be able to pull anything on you, I promise. I'm predicting ten rounds, decision your way."

Britton is at ringside, and so is Andy. Several hundred, maybe a thousand, are in the arena. Some people in the crowd are hooting.

"Hoo-hoo! Where d'ya find that short fella?" one calls.

Tommy Thompson is like a giant crane, hovering over Johnny, trying to tie him up. Johnny remembers the time he knocked out the rowdy who was harassing his father. He focuses on finding weak spots. In the first round, he sees that the guy is a swinger, and he may be ugly, but just like Britton told him, he doesn't have a plan. He's not really a boxer, but someone who throws punches wildly in the direction of his target. Johnny avoids his swings in the first round.

"You've got it, Johnny. Now pick your spot! You know how to do it!" Britton yells.

In the second round, Johnny's instincts kick in. He blocks Thompson's hits and lands a few of his own. Pretty soon, he's able to exercise control. Thompson is all over the place.

They go ten rounds. The decision is unanimous for Johnny—with $100 prize money. The announcement in the paper the next day confirms it, but to be on the safe side, he and Andy agree not to mention anything at home.

A neighbor brings over a newspaper and congratulates Rose. "That's your boy, isn't it?" she says.

Rose reads the article slowly and hands the newspaper back.

When Johnny comes home, she meets him at the door.

"After all we've done to put you through law school? And all you want is to be a prizefighter? What is wrong with you? Are you crazy?" his mother says.

"I thought I could earn a little to help—"

"Don't you know what you're doing? What's happened to you?"

"I could give boxing a try and if—"

"No, no, no, no. We will not have any part of this. This is no good for you. You, John Joseph Sirica, are *breaking* my heart. You are breaking my heart."

When Henry wires down the news that the bar results are out and that "J. Sirica" is in the pass column, Johnny knows what he has to do. He finds a freighter and boards for destinations north.

Chapter Four

A START

Law positions are not easy to find in D.C., even with a degree from Georgetown and a bar license. John knocks on doors along the 5th Street legal corridor, where all the well-known lawyers have offices—William Leahy, Frank Hogan, Alvin Newmyer, George Hoover, J. J. Darlington, Charles Fahy—but no one invites him in. Here he is, in the center of Judiciary Square, by all the courts—the police courts, the criminal courts, among the men buzzing in and out of buildings with the handles of their leather briefcases held tightly in their grip. Here he is, with a license to practice law, and nowhere to practice.

"You need to get in there and let the judges see who you are," Leo Rover tells him before they go into the Knights of Columbus gym. "You need to get some experience, get before the jury."

"I'm sorry, sir. I don't think I can. My hands shake and I start to sweat every time I stand to speak."

"You'll get over that. It's stage fright. Everyone feels it at first."

"At this rate, I don't think I'll ever have a chance," John replies, pushing open the door from the locker room. "I'm much better at boxing."

Mornings, he puts on his suit and one of his two white shirts, and sits in a row in the courtroom where lawyers fill the bench in hopes that a judge will appoint them to represent a needy client. But with a zero track record, appointments do not come his way.

Afternoons, he looks over the dockets posted by the door and drops in to watch the trial proceedings. The Teapot Dome cases are favorites. Since *The Wall Street Journal* first reported on the matter years earlier, Teapot Dome has become the greatest government scandal in the history of the nation. For the first time, a cabinet official stands accused of criminal behavior— bribery and perjury and defrauding the government, and industry titans face charges as well. The Senate investigation into the matter results in a constitutional challenge to its power to issue subpoenas, and the Supreme Court issues a definitive ruling that Congress does indeed have the power to compel testimony.

What draws John's attention, though, are the lawyers who are appearing in court. Frank Hogan and William Leahy, trial attorneys extraordinaire, are representing defendants, and John takes in each detail of how they work. They step across the courtroom in steady, measured moves; use their hands as if they are holding the keys of knowledge; speak firmly but eloquently. They seem to know exactly the right moment to object, and do so in a way that their points rise undeniably to the level of the judge.

At the gym, John describes what he sees in court, and at the same time, lets the men who come for training know about his job search. Nothing turns up. Days roll into weeks and weeks into months.

One day, a fellow named Harvey calls him over after the workout. "Got a tip for you, Johnny." He scribbles something on a piece of paper and hands it over. *Bert Emerson,* it says.

"You went to law school without a college degree, right?"

"Yes, sir. I think I was in one of the last groups they allowed to do that."

"Well, Bert Emerson did that, too, and right now, thanks to the Volstead Act and Prohibition, his business is hopping. I have a hunch that he might be to open to taking on a new hand, and he'd be sympathetic to your plight. He has a real law office—a suite with three rooms and two partners."

John turns the scrap of paper over in his hand. "I think I've seen him in arraignments."

"Everyone knows him. He's fine-tuned every method and mechanism it takes to defend a person charged with a crime in the District. I've had occasion to use him myself. Tell him I sent you. Bert might be your man."

Emerson agrees to take John on as an apprentice, and while the pay is minimal, it's a chance to be sitting in front of the "bar" that separates the lawyers on a case in the courtroom from the observers.

"Mr. Emerson says I can have a desk in his reception area," John writes to his parents. "It's not much, but it's a start."

Learning the actual practice of law is like beginning anew. Law school, John learns, has only a remote connection to the day-to-day nitty-gritty of the courts. What's more important than Latin is learning the names of the bail bondsmen and the jail visiting hours. Johnny shadows Emerson on cases and as they rush from courtroom to courtroom.

"You watch closely," Emerson whispers before he makes a motion.

John sits in the "second chair" at the defendant's table, organizing papers, helping Emerson as best he can, observing everything. He sees the way that judges manage the courtroom. In this space, there is one person in charge, and that person is in a black robe, several feet above the lawyers and everyone else. The judge is the clear authority. He's like a referee, yes, but much more—he's the governor and guiding force of the proceedings.

The D.C. criminal courts are different from others in the country because the District is part of the federal government instead of a state government. In all of the states, local prosecutors and state attorneys handle the criminal caseload for the government; in the District, the U.S. Attorney's Office for the District of Columbia represents the government. The judges are federally appointed and have tenure for life. The crimes are the same: murder, theft, extortion, vice, and lots of Prohibition violations.

John watches the way Emerson always keeps his eyes on the jury box.

"Jury psychology," Emerson tells him on the way to dinner.

"I never heard that term, sir," John says.

"Of course not. You learn theory in law school. But reading things out of books and writing answers to hypothetical questions doesn't tell you how to be a trial lawyer. That's an art. You only learn it by doing it."

"But how does psychology enter into it? It's about the facts and the law, right?"

"You have to get the jury to listen to your interpretation of the facts. 'Facts' must be proven; proof can be contested. People giving testimony put on their own spin—they rationalize things. But is it really logical? Does it really fit with the experience of the jury? You never underestimate the intelligence of the jury. You put yourself in the box as if you are one of them, and you say the things that you would want to hear. You can't give them some fantastical explanation, or just skip over things, to try to fool the jury. They're smarter than that. When you give your closing, you relate it to the testimony. For example, you say, 'You heard the testimony of the witness about x, y, and z. But does that honestly make sense?' If it seems ridiculous to you, it will seem ridiculous to the jury. You have to let them know that *you* know that *they* know just like *you* know. Psychology."

It's the week of Independence Day, July 1927, six months after John has received his bar admission certificate, when Emerson decides to go on a beach vacation far away from the cares of the court. John is assigned to go to court to cover roll call when the judge or bailiff calls the cases on the calendar, and the lawyers respond that they are present. John's job is to respond and say that Mr. Emerson is out of town, and to ask for a continuance until he returns.

One of Emerson's cases appears on the top of the calendar unexpectedly. This is a criminal case in which the defendant is charged with violation of the Prohibition laws. John closely follows the case names and docket numbers, and pops up when the case is called to request the continuance.

The judge glances down from the bench. "I don't care where Mr. Emerson is. You're here, Mr. . . ."

"Sirica. Your Honor."

"You're here, Mr. Sirica. I've seen you at the table in front of the bar, so I presume that you have actually passed the bar exam."

"Yes. But . . ." John searches the courtroom to see if one of the other lawyers in the office might be in attendance. No such luck. Of course, he should know that. They've all left their calendars for him to answer at roll call.

"You've been sitting here for months, Mr. Sirica. Now do something. Find your client and let's get going."

John motions to the client, perched in the back row, and begins fumbling through Emerson's folder. The client has been caught cold-handed selling liquor by an undercover officer. A jury is selected. There is barely any testimony—the agent describes how the client poured bootleg liquor for him at the client's candy stand. The agent arrested him and found a barrel behind the counter. A police expert testifies that, after testing, it is indeed determined to be alcohol. A photographer testifies that he took a picture of the defendant, giving the liquor to the agent. The defendant testifies that he didn't know it was liquor. The trial is over before noon, and the jury takes only ten minutes to reach a verdict and find the defendant guilty.

"Do you want to put the sentencing on the calendar or do it now?" the judge asks.

John tries to remember a similar situation that Emerson has handled. What would his more experienced colleague do? What's the psychology here?

"Now, Your Honor."

"Very well. It's an open-and-closed case. Direct flouting of the law. The defendant knew exactly what he was doing, and I see no reason for leniency. I sentence him to six years in prison. Bailiff, remand the defendant to prison immediately."

John blinks as they handcuff Emerson's client and march him away.

When Emerson returns, he consoles John. "If it were me, John, I would postpone the sentencing. The judge might cool down, and the defendant can prepare some kind of case. Maybe you can scare up some letters in support of the defendant, from his pastor or a neighbor or a business association. Or show he's the sole provider of children. Offer something—that's the trick."

"I wasn't thinking about the strategy, the plan. I had no idea." John puts his head in his hands.

"Let's get them now, and maybe we can seek a sentence reduction. Can't hurt to try."

"Yes, sir. I'll get right on that."

John writes his parents, if not with all of the details, at least the one fact that might make them happy.

> *Dear Mother and Father, I had my first jury trial this week. It's a start.*

Smaller cases are handed over to John when Emerson is too busy—or too hung over, which is not infrequent. A few cases come directly to John from connections he's made at the gym. When one case gets a mention in the *Evening Star*, he clips the story. It's only 1.5 inches, stuck in the bottom corner, but he puts it into an envelope and addresses it to his mother, underlining his name with a black pen.

"Wife Sues for Divorce," says the headline, under which it reads: "Harry H. Curtis, retired sergeant U.S.A., and a watchman at the Munitions Building, was sued for limited divorce yesterday by his wife, Ida May Curtis, on charges of cruelty and non-support. Attorney John J. Sirica appeared for the wife."

Soon, there's a four-inch clipping, from the middle of the page: "Rum Possession Charges Upheld: Gaming Table Count Dismissed." The story explains that the proprietors of a cigar store face charges of illegal possession of two thousand quarts of whiskey found in a garage behind their establishment. The arresting officers also put in an additional charge of gaming: "In the rear room of the store, racing slips were found, along with a telephone with a direct connection to the race track," the article states. "Attorney John J. Sirica obtained the dismissal of the gaming charge, and will go to trial on the illegal possession charges. His clients contend they had no knowledge of the liquor." The article also makes note of the prosecuting attorney—R. P. Camalier—which might impress his mother, too. The Camalier family is known throughout the District for its long-established roots and prominent connections.

John avoids sending his mother any updates about his boxing exploits. He's at the Knights of Columbus gym daily, and every now and then agrees to a fight at a club, although he's careful to have a "cover" name. He's fighting with an eight-ounce glove now. He's never nervous when boxing, never frightened. He gets in the ring, takes stock of his opponent, and creates a fight plan in his mind. Sometimes there are hundreds of people watching the club fights, but they don't bother him at all. The more he boxes, the more confident he becomes—in the ring and in the courtroom, too.

At night, he searches out witnesses for cases or accompanies Emerson on his travels around the city, always aware that his mentor might need a little help getting home if he's has an extra swig or two.

One night, the duo stops for dinner at a favorite D.C. spot and spreads out interview notes at the table, when a man in a suit approaches.

"You're Italian, aren't you?" the man says to John.

"Why do you ask?" John puts his pencil down. His legs stiffen under the table, and he prepares to push back his chair.

The man hands him a card: *Ralph Cipriano, New York Life Insurance.*

"I heard the waiter call you Mr. Silisa, and I can't help but think that—"

"Sirica. The name is Johnny Sirica. If you're out to sell insurance, I can save you some time, Ralph. I'm not in the market. But if you need a lawyer, have a seat."

"You *are* Italian! And a lawyer!" Cipriano pulls up a chair. "The reason I ask . . . a group of us are forming a civic club for businessmen and professionals of Italian descent and—"

"What's the group? What's it trying to do?" Now that John is in the criminal defense field, he's constantly trying to get underneath what people are saying.

"We want to highlight positive contributions of Italian Americans in Washington D.C. to combat prejudice," Cipriano says. "We're having a meeting on Tuesday. If you're interested, I'd like to invite you as my guest."

Emerson, sitting across from John, silently nods. John reaches out and shakes Cipriano's hand.

Chapter Five

AN ITALIAN FELLOWSHIP

Nearly a dozen men gather at the Nobile Restaurant on E Street on November 19, 1929. Despite the stock market crash only two weeks earlier, animated voices fill the back room. Ralph Cipriano brings John over to Massimo Ferrari and Fedele Colaprico—the two other organizers of the event.

"And this little fellow," Cipriano says of John, "is a dynamo lawyer."

"We've got some rules to draw up and sure could use another legal mind. Sit down, John," Ferrari says.

Ferrari taps his spoon on a glass to get the group's attention and projects loudly so he can be heard at the other end of the table.

"Welcome, one and all," he says. "We're here in fellowship. We're here as the sons of Italian men who came to this country to build a new life. We're proud of our Italian heritage and we're proud Americans. But if you're like me, you've noticed there's a pattern of negative stories about Italians in D.C. and in the country in general. Ugly and untrue stereotypes find their way into the public commons, and the good that we are doing gets lost. We need to do more to share the positive contributions of Italian men and to build valuable relations in the community. That's why Fedele and Ralph and I called us all together."

The men rap their knuckles on the table in agreement.

John studies the faces. He recognizes several from the newspapers. He can't wait to tell his father—doctors, businessmen, former military officers, government officials. And him—Johnny Sirica. All Italian.

John's never thought of himself as Italian so much as American. And a patriotic American, at that. But he still shudders to think of the names he's been called, the Benny German types who exude disdain, and the discrimination his father has faced. An organization that will lift up the good works of Italian Americans seems like an excellent idea.

Cipriano takes over now. "We've got big plans. We want to raise money for scholarships for immigrants and raise funds for people who experience catastrophes. We'll be here to give a proper greeting to Italian dignitaries who come to Washington. As we help our community and spread the good word, so we'll help ourselves as well."

"I have a name!" calls a robust man, introduced as Dr. Raphael Manganaro. "Lido. Let's call it the Lido Civic Club. Everyone loves the Lido in Venice. What in Italy is more beautiful than Venice, and what in Venice is more Italian than the Lido? You want to restore your health? Go to the beach at Lido! Need a place to gather with colleagues? The beach at Lido! For centuries," he says. "Plus, it has the best gelato."

The men around the table shout cheers and raise their glasses.

"Lido! Everyone in agreement?" asks Ferrari.

The knocks on the table create an indoor thunder.

"Lido Civic Club it is!" says Ferrari. "Tell the waiter: gelato all around!"

The club begins to take shape. It will have a symbol: the Lion of St. Mark the Evangelist since, like an evangelist, they will be spreading good news. They add an inscription: *Paz Tibi Marc Evangelista Meus*—"Peace to you, O Mark, My Evangelist."

By early December, Lido has a constitution, a charter, and thirty founding members. To John, it's more than a professional group, and even more than a way to build connections—it's family. He lets people know he's willing to step in the ring for president in the next club election. Another first for him.

The club gives him more courage to put himself forward in other ways, too, as does Bert Emerson. From the moment that Leo Rover is named by President Hoover to be the U.S. attorney for the entire District of Columbia, Emerson prods John.

"Ask him for a job," Emerson says as they wait for the calendar call at the courthouse.

John's been in Emerson's office for nearly three years. He's handled dozens of small-potatoes cases that the other attorneys don't want, and has been appointed by the court on fourteen felony matters. But with the economy the way it is, it's getting harder and harder for people to pay their legal bills. A government job would mean a steady paycheck—and on the staff of the prosecutor's office, John might be able to save up some money, even help his parents out.

As the after-effects of the stock market crash start multiplying in the spring, John works up his courage to talk to Leo Rover when they are lacing up for a workout at the gym.

"I'd like to ask, Mr. Rover, if you might consider me for an opening at the U.S. attorney's office, should one arise."

"Let me tell you, John, I already have it in mind. You don't have to ask again. I'd like to have you as a trial assistant when the time is right. You've really built up the experience and learned the ropes. That's what we need. You know how to stand on your own two feet in court now—just about as well as you know how to box. That's an accomplishment, and don't think I haven't noticed."

Toward the summer of 1930, Assistant U.S. Attorney William A. Gallagher gives John a call.

"Mr. Rover asked me to contact you. He said to tell you he has an opening and he'd like to appoint you. Are you interested?"

"Yes, sir. Very much so," John says, breathing deeply as he takes in the next set of instructions.

"Mr. Rover said to tell you that before he can put your name in, you need to get letters of endorsement from two Republicans. Officeholders are good. The higher up in office, the better. Senators, perhaps," says Gallagher.

"Yes, sir, I'll do that," John responds.

He hangs up. The fact is he doesn't know any Republicans. His parents, when they are political, are Democrats. Right now, they are *very* political—his father hates Hoover and makes no bones about it. Catholics are especially downcast about the Republicans after a wave of anti-Catholic smears finishes off the presidential hopes of Democrat Al Smith in 1928.

John hasn't paid much attention to the political parties. The District of Columbia doesn't even have senators in Congress.

Now politics—and politicians—are suddenly the linchpin of his future.

After running through his D.C. contacts without success, John hits on the idea of getting in touch with Fonsy, now back in Waterbury. He splurges on a long-distance phone call.

"Do you know any Republicans?" The urgency in John's voice is palpable.

"Are you a Republican?" Fonsy asks.

"I am now," says John, laughing a bit.

Fonsy mentions that his sister Gertrude serves on a local Republican committee. John immediately boards a train to Waterbury to seek her help.

Gertrude, now married to a Dr. Bowes in Waterbury, agrees to do what she can. She starts going through her connections, and they pay off. U.S. Representative Ned Goss agrees to write a letter on John's behalf, and then Connecticut's Senator Harry Bingham says that he will, too.

"I was offered the appointment!" John writes to Gertrude and Fonsy two weeks later, careful to splash extra ink from his fountain pen on the exclamation mark. "I am officially a Republican. For life. No changing teams for me. This is it! I will never forget the chance these men took on me. Thank you, my cousins!"

Being an assistant United States attorney carries many responsibilities—but it's a lot less stressful than being a defense attorney and wondering if the client will show up in court or will be able to pay his attorney bill if he does. The prosecutor has more control—whom to charge, what to charge. Police officers do the investigations rather than John having to drive around neighborhoods at night looking for witnesses. There are experts on tap to testify. The whole weight of the government is behind each decision.

Still, putting together a solid case takes long hours and in-depth preparation. The prosecutor is responsible for proving the case and for telling a cohesive story that doesn't overwhelm the jury. With the local criminal blotter as his field of operation, all kinds of matters immediately come to John's desk.

When John is handed the homicide prosecution of Albert C. Baker in 1931, he reads through the police records methodically. Baker is arrested after his wife, Anna, is found dead at his home on O Street. The two had separated, and their three children were living in the home with Albert. Anna had taken to coming to the home in Albert's absence to look after the children. When Albert returned home early one day and found her, he demanded that she return permanently to take care of him. She refused, and he shot her in the back. Anna died before an ambulance could get her to the hospital.

John files a charge of first-degree murder and tries it to a jury. The jurors instead come back with conviction on second-degree murder. The defendant's lawyer asks for the minimum sentence of twenty years while John asks the judge for the maximum sentence to put the man away for as long as possible.

"Shooting someone in the back? Shooting a mother in front of her children? The depravity in this crime is extraordinary, Your Honor, and demands nothing less than the maximum penalty under the law," John tells the judge hearing the case.

The defense attorney has his own argument: Baker should get the minimum so he can take care of the three children, he says.

"That's outrageous," John retorts, speaking out from the prosecution table before the defense attorney even finishes his argument. "That's like the old saw about the boy who kills his parents and then asks for mercy on the grounds that he is an orphan. I urge the court to flatly reject this line of nonsense."

The judge takes the matter under advisement. He comes back with the sentencing disposition five days later: the minimum sentence, as the defense has requested.

Back at the prosecutor's office, John rushes to see Rover.

"How can that be fair to the public? To the people?" John demands, although he is not really expecting an answer. "The wife is dead. The man killed her. If a man commits a crime, he should pay for it."

"Of course. But don't let your temper get the better of you. That's our system, and we have to live with it."

"One thing I can tell ya," John says, clenching his fist and letting it land lightly on the desk. "If I were the judge, he'd have gotten the maximum. The public needs to know that crime will be punished severely."

"Yes, my friend, that's the benefit of being the one to wear the robe. You're only, what . . . twenty-seven years old? But maybe someday, it will be your turn."

Chapter Six

A FRIEND FOR LIFE

When Republican Herbert Hoover loses to Democrat Franklin Delano Roosevelt in 1932, John sees what's coming. The trouble with jobs that arise from political appointments is that they can also end with a shift in political winds. In December 1933, the other shoe drops. Leo Rover is replaced by Roosevelt's pick, Leslie C. Garnett, and John and the other attorneys in the division pack up their desks.

With Thomas Scalley, another struggling lawyer, John hangs a shingle in a little two-room office on 15th Street NW. The rent is $90 a month, and a secretary makes $10 a week. The two lawyers, together, barely scrape by.

To stretch his budget, John lives with his parents, who've moved back to D.C. and are residing in a modest home in the northwest. While working at the office of the U.S. attorney, John had helped them to buy the house in a new development at Sheridan and 14th Street NW when it was still under construction—the first time that Fred and Rose Sirica would be able to own a home of their own.

Before completion of the house, Fred and Rose had received a certified letter from the developer, saying the contract was being cancelled.

John finds the developer's office. "How do you explain this?" he demands.

The builder hems and haws. "Nothing against your folks, you see. But I got some complaints."

"Complaints about what?" asks John. His parents haven't even moved in.

"It's a problem for some of the real estate people who sell in the neighborhood. What can I say? I'm sure another nice property will come up in the District."

"What type of problem?" John stares directly at the builder.

"You know, some of these real estate people—narrow-minded. They see the name on the purchase, they don't want to list the Sheridan properties. They think the neighborhood will become too Italian, some such thing. So I gotta do what I what gotta do to protect the development. Big investment for me."

"Too many Italians are 'invading the area'?" John doesn't hide his sarcasm as he repeats a phrase the Lido Civic Club members have seen in anti-Italian screeds posted on bulletin boards and empty store windows.

"I'm not saying I agree with them. I mean, you know, I was forced into this position. Didn't want to. Was forced."

"Over my dead body." John holds the contract firmly in front of the builder with both hands. "It's a good contract. And there is no clause in it that allows it to be cancelled because of a bunch of narrow-minded realtors. You can honor it—or we can go to court, which, I don't mind telling you, is something that I enjoy quite a bit."

Ten days later, Fred and Rose get another certified letter, telling them to ignore the first certified letter and giving them a move-in date.

In the first month after they settle in, Fred plants a rose garden out front. Suddenly, the realtors are walking prospective buyers past their property to promote the development.

A place to live is one thing, but building a law practice from scratch seems nearly impossible. John makes the rounds—to the Lido Civic Club, the local bar association, the John Carroll Society of Catholic professionals. He passes out his card and sends congratulatory notes to friends, but there is no getting around the Great Recession. Clients are sparse.

In October of 1934, boxing promoter Goldie Ahearn bursts into John's office first thing in the morning.

"Johnny, grab your jacket. They want you at the courthouse."

A former boxer who earned a title in the military, Ahearn quit his pro career after a nasty bout in 1926. Now he owns a haberdashery shop in the District and is a man-about-town— he knows everyone, especially in sporting circles, and everyone knows him.

"Who wants me?"

"Arraignment. Samuel Beard! He wants someone who's got experience inside the federal prosecutor's office, and that's you. They sent a man up to my shop to get you."

John stuffs a pad in his briefcase, makes sure he has the

numbers of a few bail bondsmen, and heads out, reading the newspaper as he walks.

"Gambling King Caught in Raid on Horse Race Center," it says. The prosecutors say that Beard is the kingpin of an intricate underground gambling operation, and they aim to clean up the District. Beard's raided office had forty phones with forty lines, and was connected to dozens of bookie houses. To nab him, the investigators moved a government agent into an adjacent office and put a wiretap on his phone lines.

At trial, Beard says that he was only giving out real-time race information, not taking bets. John argues that there is no proof implicating his client, and that the police, under pressure to make arrests, used improper methods.

In page-one coverage of the trial, the newspaper reads: "Sirica closes his case by waxing indignant over the harassment of his client. 'If there ever were a case where the Police Department brought its dirty linen to the District Attorney's Office, this is it,'" Sirica tells the jury.

Despite his "waxing," Beard is convicted.

And even with a headline criminal matter, John is still scrambling to make ends meet.

Ahearn has a proposition. "They're legalizing boxing in the District, so we need to get going with professional boxers—the top-notch ones. Get some fights going."

The ban on professional boxing in D.C. is finally ending in 1934—although it has taken an act of Congress to make it happen.

"What're ya thinking?" John asks.

"You and me. We know boxing in and out. We can get in on the ground floor, open an arena, get in some headliners. We'll make a bundle of money. Think what it would be like if we had Max Baer or Jimmy Braddock, right here. People would come out in droves."

"You think we can pull it together?"

"You and me, Johnny—we'll be rolling in dough."

They start meeting daily at John's office. They form a corporation and locate a venue. But the big names aren't interested—they want to see if pro boxing in D.C. is going to catch on. The fighters who are willing to go on the cards aren't the ones who are going to draw a crowd.

One morning, John twirls a pencil over his list of names during his meeting with Ahearn. "No one is jumping out," he says.

"What we're gonna do, Johnny—we're going to get Dempsey," Ahearn announces while biting into a sandwich.

"Quit playing, Goldie. You know as well as I do, he's not fighting anymore." John hesitates for a moment. "Although, if he were . . ." he trails off.

Back in 1921 when he was finishing up Columbia Prep, John had seen Dempsey in person as the then-champ jogged along the beach early mornings in Atlantic City. Dempsey was preparing for his big fight with the French champion Georges Carpentier—"the battle of the century." Johnny was working the night shift as a clerk at the Terminal Hotel in Atlantic City and helping his folks run the vacation rental they were trying to operate. Watching Dempsey's determination spurred John to begin his own training regime and to shed his roly-poly fat. No, it wasn't an exaggeration to say he idolized Dempsey, even if he didn't care to share all of that with Ahearn.

"Sure, it would be swell to have Dempsey," John says,

tapping his pencil. "But he hasn't fought since '27 against Gene Tunney. Dempsey's still the champ, if you ask me, but he's in the movies now. Did you see him in *The Prizefighter and the Lady*?"

"Officiating! We're going to get him to referee, like he did in that *Prizefighter* movie, and everyone will want to see Dempsey! 'Dempsey! Dempsey!' We'll promote that Jack Dempsey will be here. Tickets will be flying off the counter. I got a friend, Maxie Waxman, in New York who's doing Dempsey's business management."

"If you think it'll work. I hawked 'Extra! Dempsey Wins!' as a newsboy. Imagine that. Yeah, let's get Dempsey."

Ahearn's crazy scheme brings Dempsey to the District. As soon as the boxer arrives, Ahearn brings him right to John's office to show how legitimate they are.

"A lawyer," Dempsey says. "In my world, I run into a lot of people needing a good lawyer."

"Didn't plan it this way, but boxing gave me the courage to stand up in court," John says. "Nothing like you, of course, but I had a couple of pro matches—here, Florida. Not sure it's exactly a selling point for most clients." He motions to Dempsey to sit in one of the two client chairs.

"Someone little as you must know how to pack a punch!" Dempsey thrusts his fist outward, the way photographers always want him to pose, and laughs at his own comment. "You got to have confidence in yourself, kid. You have to say you're the best, and then live up to it. None of this waffling about. That ain't credible."

"Grew up hardscrabble—it's tough to leave behind," says John.

"You haven't seen hardscrabble 'til you seen Manassa,

Colorado. A bunch of miners . . . and let's just say you think twice before crossing them. Why do you think I took up boxing, John? Now, come on, you're going to make it big someday. I got a feelin' in my bones."

John's face turns red. No one—not even Leo Rover or Bert Emerson or Jack Britton or Morris Cafritz or his cousin Fonsy or his own father—has given him a pep talk like this, like he's standing there in the corner for you, even when you're on the ropes.

"If you think so . . . ."

"'Call it like you see it'—that's my motto." Dempsey snaps his finger and points to the floor like a ref. "And I'm calling it."

"Well . . . thank you. Thank you, Mr. Dempsey."

"Call me Jack! We're pals. You come to New York, meet some of my buddies up there. I'll take you to the Stork Club. And El Morocco. We're going to show you around, Johnny. Never made it past eighth grade myself. But you—a boxer *and* a lawyer— that's something." He holds out his palm and John grabs it into a long handshake, rough surfaces comfortably aligned.

Despite Ahearn's fervent promotion of Dempsey, the box office receipts don't add up the way he'd predicted. The boxing promotion business goes on hiatus. So far, in the Sirica family, only the taxi service run by John's brother Andy seems to have anything close to a moneymaking touch.

John keeps working all the angles. Leo Rover contacts him about getting involved with the Republican Committee for the District of Columbia.

"We're headed to Cleveland for the Republican Convention,

and I need people on my team to fight before the Credentials Committee. Are you up for it?" Rover says. "We're going to win back the White House."

"I'm going get me one of those straw convention hats at Goldie Ahearn's shop," John says. "You bet I'm up for it."

More than 17,000 Republicans from across the country cram into the Cleveland Convention Hall. Red, white, and blue bunting circles the podium; convention-goers are squeezed into every corner. Thick smoke fills the air as attendees puff away at cigarettes and cigars.

The convention is intent on bringing back a "return to the fundamental principles of our government." When ex-president Herbert Hoover arrives, conventioneers erupt with wild cheering.

"Franklin Delano Roosevelt and his 'New Deal' are driving the country in the wrong direction," Hoover declares, and the crowd rises in a frenzy.

In the end, Kansas governor Alfred Landon takes the nomination, but it's the camaraderie and jostling with political fellows that sticks with John. He feels that he belongs, and it has not gone without notice that politicians are key players in naming judges, especially in the District of Columbia.

After Landon loses, John runs for the D.C. Republican Committee. He takes to the road when Wendell Willkie is the Republican nominee in 1940, visiting Italian-American groups up and down the East Coast and delivering stump speeches for the candidate.

Roosevelt's unprecedented third term puts most D.C. government jobs out of reach. But the ever-widening circle of contacts is paying off.

One afternoon, the phone rings in John's office. He waits a moment before picking up.

"Sirica," he says.

"Met you at the Stork Club in New York. Jack Dempsey was taking you around, as I recall. Is that right?"

John instantly recognizes the caller and sits up straight in his chair. Who wouldn't know the voice of Walter Winchell, the high-intensity, fast-moving, no-nonsense reporter—the most famous and notorious news personality in the country? Twenty-five million people listen to him on the radio, tuning in each Sunday night at nine—and John is one of them. He reads Winchell's syndicated column, too. The legendary reporter holds Table No. 50 in the elite private room of the Stork Club, John recalls.

Winchell continues. "This crazy publisher in Washington is suing me for libel because I said her publication is a piece of garbage not even fit for wrapping fish, or some such thing. Which it is. I need someone scrappy to represent me in a lawsuit. Someone who knows the street." Winchell, true to his radio persona, maintains his rat-a-tat delivery. "I don't intend to pay her a dollar. Not a dime. Not a penny. I will see that attorneys' fees are fully paid, whatever it takes. Are you up for the fight?"

The lawsuit in federal district court is filed by Mrs. Eleanor M. Patterson—everyone calls her "Cissy"—owner and publisher of the *Washington Times-Herald*. Patterson's complaint says that Winchell's broadcast on March 15, 1942, referred to her with "false, scandalous, malicious, and defamatory words." For this, she is seeking $400,000 in damages—$100,000 each against radio show sponsor Andrew Jergens Co. and the network National Broadcasting Company, or its successor The Blue Network, and $200,000 against Winchell.

John unravels the whole sequence of events. It seems that the broadcast in question began with a story about George Sylvester

Viereck, an American supporter of the Nazis who was on trial in D.C. for being an unregistered foreign agent. Winchell is avid in his anti-Nazi beliefs. In his rapid-fire commentary on Viereck's trial, Winchell noted that Viereck was a close friend of a U.S. senator who was a strong supporter of Germany, and that senator was so enamored with an editorial on foreign policy in the *Washington Times-Herald* that he read it into the Congressional Record.

In response, Patterson reran her editorial—it was about why the U.S. should occupy Greenland to protect it from a Nazi invasion. She added a footnote about Winchell's commentary, saying that she was proud of the editorial and sometimes it is necessary to "squash a cockroach." With that, she sued Winchell.

John pushes every legal avenue on the Winchell case. He means to win this one. After ten months, Patterson's lawyers drop the claims against the sponsor and the network, and offer to settle with Winchell for $25,000.

"Not one penny," Winchell repeats.

John declines the offer and announces that he is ready to go to trial.

On the trial date in May 1943, John, with Winchell at his side, addresses the judge. "I do note that Mrs. Patterson, the plaintiff, is not in the courtroom. I make a motion for an immediate and complete dismissal of this matter."

The plaintiff's attorney clears his throat. "Mr. Winchell admitted in a deposition that the editorial in question is a very patriotic piece and disclaimed any intention to besmirch the *Times-Herald*. Furthermore, Winchell's contract with his radio sponsor allows him to escape any judgment. As a result, Mrs. Patterson does not feel any good purpose will be served in further prosecuting the case." The lawyer sits.

"Case dismissed," announces the judge. He bangs the gavel and heads back to his chambers.

Winchell slaps John on the back. "Complete victory! You've done it, my man! Not one penny!"

When the check for payment arrives, John banks the largest fee he's earned to date: $25,000. There's another bonus as well. Winchell introduces him to his friends on Capitol Hill and beyond—people like the politician Joe McCarthy from Wisconsin and U.S. Representative Clarence Lea of California—Republicans and Democrats alike.

Chapter Seven

A WHITEWASH

John carefully fills out each line in the personal history form for the general counsel position at the Congressional Select Committee to Investigate the Federal Communications Commission (FCC). In 1944, he's been ten years without a regular paycheck, drinking one cup of Sanka after another while waiting for the office phone to ring. A job on the Hill is definitely appealing.

He duly notes the towns in Italy where his grandparents were born; the date four years earlier when his father died, too young, after a heart attack; his mother's address in D.C., where he still lives. If he can get this job, he might be able to afford an apartment of his own.

Rep. Clarence Lea, a Democrat, had called him in a panic for this job. The House Select Committee was in a jam.

"I need someone who can't be shaken like the last General Counsel," said Lea. "You're a straight shooter who knows how to get the evidence on the table. I need someone to come in and handle these hearings. As soon as possible."

Things had become messy at the committee investigating the FCC. The former chair of the committee and the one who initiated the hearings, Rep. Eugene Cox of Georgia, was no longer on the committee. He'd been forced off amid allegations of conflict of interest and potential ethics violations for having accepted a fee to represent a constituent before the FCC. The prior general counsel—Wall Street lawyer and ardent anti-Communist Eugene Carey—had left the post suddenly for unspecified reasons, although rumors swirled that some higher-ups threatened to disclose nefarious activities of a friend unless he stepped down.

The FCC was a New Deal hot potato. Conservatives hated the new commission because of the way it had been given power to regulate the expanding radio industry and to grant—or deny—lucrative radio licenses. With 980 stations in 1944, radio was making money, buckets of it—and the future looked even more promising. Initially regulated by the Department of Commerce, radio operations were consolidated with telephone technology, and oversight was placed in the hands of the new FCC, an independent agency, in 1934.

Now, less than a decade later, the FCC found itself mired in controversy.

Twenty-four allegations of fraud and manipulation at the FCC kick off the hearings. Soon, there are fifty charges. Rep. Cox, the first chair, calls the FCC one of the "nastiest rats" of the New Deal. He says it centralizes federal power, erodes individual liberties, uses fascist tactics, and is filled with Communists.

There are rumors of cronyism and payoffs, misspent monies, and insider decisions of favor and fear. Under the driving force of Rep. Cox and General Counsel Carey, subpoenas fly, and thousands upon thousands of documents are demanded from the FCC. Most attention is directed to questions about the sale of station WMCA in New York. The prior owner says he was intimidated into selling his station. There are allegations of involvement by high-ranking government officials and lobbyists—maybe even FDR's freewheeling son, Elliott Roosevelt.

The former general counsel considers everything to be fair play. He sends multiple investigators to root out a possible romance of the FCC head, and demands travel receipts from all staffers. The communications industry magazine, *Billboard*, refers to it as "unimpartial probing."

The new chair—Rep. Lea—is eager to get back on track. He and John agree to put aside the Communist allegations and personal issues, and to look at relevant facts.

John digs in and finds a tangled web that points to the questionable handling of radio transfers. There's a strong case of wrongdoing related to the case of WMCA, a leading station in New York City, operating from atop the Hotel McAlpin at Herald Square. It's known for its broadcasts of music, radio dramas, and New York Giants baseball games. Owner Donald Flamm built the station from its beginnings in 1925. He gave up the license in 1940 to Edward J. Noble, the former Undersecretary of Commerce under FDR, but claims he did so only under duress. He says powerful men told him that if he didn't sell, the FCC would strip his license and he'd lose everything.

The sale involved many political heavyweights. The deal was handled by the former chief counsel to the FCC, William Dempsey, who happened to share an office with "Tommy the Cork" Corcoran, close friends with FDR and a political "fixer." Flamm had previously turned down an offer from Elliott

Roosevelt, but under pressure, hastily sold the station at 68 percent of its value. A group of investors quickly flipped it for double that amount.

John's investigation identifies a potent list of people ready to testify. One man is willing to say under oath that he was part of a conspiracy to force a turnover of the license.

As the hearings reconvene, Rep. Lea calls John over to his office.

"You're doing a great job as general counsel, John. Everything I thought should happen, you've done." He offers John a hard candy from a bowl.

"I think you're going to be impressed with the quality of the testimony coming up, sir," John replies, taking a candy.

"I expect I will." Rep. Lea stands up, then sits back down, rubbing his forehead. "Listen, there's been a bit of a change. Nothing that will affect your work specifically. But I thought you should be made aware of it. The committee is going to take a vote tomorrow, and I don't have the support to stop it."

"Stop what?"

"Based on my assessment of the situation, the majority of the committee is going to vote to close the rest of the hearings to the public."

John moves to the edge of his chair and leans across the large desk. "Mr. Representative, that's completely wrong. These are matters of public interest. The people have a right to know."

"I agree. I think it's unfortunate. But except for one other member, everyone on the committee is going the other way," says Lea.

"Why? Because they don't want to hear about a conspiracy to force Flamm to sell? Or because it points to powerful men who were part of the administration? People who acted with FCC assent?"

"Well, Mr. Noble says that the notion of a conspiracy is absurd. And he's a very credible person, knows a lot of people. Some of the committee members believe that we should leave the testimony to the civil courts. That's what they tell me." Lea spins slightly in his chair, keeping his eyes on John.

"People at the top pressured a man to sell off private property—with the help of the government. That needs to be exposed!" John bellows now, and is surprised to hear it himself. "We're talking about members of the commission, former officers, people who are sworn to work for the people of the country, not their own private interests. This is sensational testimony! You know that. These investors may have been in cahoots with the son of the—"

"I'm going to propose that we will release the information later. That's the best that I can do. For now, the committee wants to close the hearings."

"Behind closed doors—that's the best way to cover up foul deeds, isn't it? Can you look me in the eye and guarantee that there will be a public release?" John stares squarely at Lea.

"Some of it, I'm sure will be public. I promise you that. I mean, I convinced you to come on over and do this investigation. I'm on your side, John." Lea fiddles with a handkerchief in his pocket. "But I also need to warn you . . . some of the testimony—the WMCA testimony—is going to be sealed."

"So that no one will ever hear the truth!" John stands abruptly.

"I will talk to them again about the importance of public release," Lea replies.

"People in high places don't get a free pass to violate the law," says John. "My father taught me that. The Teapot Dome taught us all that! High rollers or low rollers, everyone should pay the price for their misdeeds, and the price should be the same for one and all. This isn't about Democrats or Republicans. This is about the Constitution of the United States of America. This is what makes our country great. This is why people come from all over the world to live here."

"I wanted you to hear it from me rather than getting blindsided in the committee room."

John composes himself. "Thank you, sir. I will respond appropriately," he says, then scribbles some notes on the inside flap of a folder.

The next day in the hearing room, a motion is made to close the hearings. Rep. Lea opposes it, as does one of the Republican members. They lose.

"Motion passed. This will be the last open session of the committee," says Rep. Lea to the reporters and observers. "I think it unwise and imprudent, but the vote is cast."

John stands. "I have a statement that I'd like to read into the record, Mr. Chairman."

"Very well," says Rep. Lea.

Some of the newsmen who are following the hearings quickly flip to a new page in their pads.

"There is only one way I can try a case, whether before a congressional committee or in a courtroom, and that is to present all the facts and let the chips fall where they may," John says. "There is great public interest in this case. I know what is going to happen and I don't want it on my conscience. No one can say that John J. Sirica, a resident of the District for many years, is party to a whitewash. Accordingly, I resign."

~

The Congressional Select Committee to Investigate the Federal Communications Commission releases a report the next year. The WMCA testimony is sealed; no wrongdoing is reported.

John orders a copy of the blue bound final report of the committee and keeps it within arm's reach on his bookshelf.

"Whitewash," he says to visitors to his office, pointing to the volume. "You want to know what a cover-up looks like? All you need to do is read that volume from the House of Representatives: 'Study and Investigation of the Federal Communications Commission: Investigation of Radio Station WMCA.' Your one hundred percent classic whitewash. Anyone with two eyes can see it, even with the evidence sealed. And I saw it for myself."

Chapter Eight

THE WHITE-COLLAR LAW

John takes off his hat as he enters the Federal District Court, ready to file papers for a client.

"Sirica! John Sirica!"

John looks around and sees Frank J. Hogan waving. Everyone in the District's legal circles knows Hogan as a crackerjack lawyer. He heads Hogan & Hartson, a powerhouse law firm in D.C.

"Yes, sir," John nods.

"You're here!"

"Yes, sir."

"Folks have been telling me you're traveling. On the big stage, or some such thing."

"Oh, that. I do travel around with Jack Dempsey, sir. We go all around, stumping for war bonds, trying to get people to sign up. We put on a little dog-and-pony show. I interview him on stage: How did he learn to punch? How did he win his first big title fight? What makes his hook so good? Leading questions, you might say. He answers them all, telling a few jokes along the way. The audience eats it up. Then he pitches government bonds, and people actually line up to buy them. Crazy thing. Richmond, Louisville, Fort Lauderdale, New Orleans, Detroit, Chicago. Minneapolis—we met the mayor, Hubert Humphrey. In Milwaukee, a candidate for the Senate showed us around. San Francisco, Arizona, you name it. But that's a couple years back—'45, '46."

"Good, good. Now you're back in town?"

"Back in town, back in court."

John starts fiddling with his folder. He's eager to get it to the clerk's office, and he's not sure what this is about, but Hogan isn't someone to ignore. He's admired Hogan ever since he watched him and William Leahy in the Teapot Dome cases twenty years back. He can even remember meeting up with Henry Jawish one night and telling him about Hogan and Leahy's courtroom feats: "When it seems like they're trapped, there's no way out, they come up with something new—feint a little, bob, pull a one-two. Cool as cucumbers. This is an art, Henry, a true art."

Now, in 1948, Hogan & Hartson is the largest firm in D.C. It specializes in cases that fall in the crossroads of government and business—a growing sector with all of the New Deal agencies.

"Still representing the King?" Hogan asks John in the hallway.

The crinkles around John's eyes tighten and he shakes his head. "Oh, so you remember Sam Beard? Gambling king. Not exactly your type of case, is it?"

"Front page. High pressure. Lots of evidence."

"I'm doing more civil cases now." John holds up the folder. "About to file one, in fact."

"We're looking for a fresh face for our litigation and criminal defense division," Hogan says. "White collar. We have the oil and gas companies. Civil litigation that needs a strategic thinker. Case of bribery here and there. Contracts. Insurance claims. Big mix. We need someone who can find his way around the local courthouse without a map. I've been keeping my eye on you. I want you to come around and meet the partners."

At age forty-four, John is weary of the life of a solo practitioner. He's all but given up on a big-firm slot with all their emphasis on the legacy hires—the elite boys from upscale families and Mayflower credentials. His ambition has turned in other directions. He and office mate Tom Scalley fantasize about judgeships—lifetime appointments in D.C.

John slips his fingers along the rim of the hat he holds in one hand. "I'm going to be doing some campaigning for the Republican ticket in '48," he says.

"That won't be an obstacle. I've seen your name on the literature from the Republican Club, so I know where you're coming from," Hogan tells him. "In fact, the partners might see it as a plus."

John takes in all of the details when he visits the Hogan offices. A reception area. With a staff. A conference room. A library. Secretarial help. Investigators. Assistant lawyers, transcribers. Free coffee. A title: senior attorney.

Hogan takes him around personally. They make John an offer within days; the generous proposed annual salary of $17,000 guarantees that he will accept.

Sitting in his new office, John likes the way his name looks embossed on the Hogan & Hartson stationery. He's gotten very good at the art of letter writing—lessons from Leo Rover. John spends an hour each morning dictating letters to people he's met— at a meeting of the Lido Civic Club, golfing, on Capitol Hill, at

Republican Party events. He writes to the people who appear in his daily review of the newspapers: *"Good luck," "Best wishes on your retirement," "So happy to hear about your recent award."*

And he writes to his best friend:

Dear Jack:

I see where you have been voted the Greatest Boxer of the Half-Century by sportswriters. No vote could be more accurate. You are not only a great boxer, but people can learn a lot from observing the way you treat people. We sure saw that on our war bonds tour! You are still the idol of millions, and you will always be the Champ to me. Come visit us anytime at Hogan!

Your pal,
Johnny.

File folders are dropped into an inbox in the center of his desk. Insurance claims by freighters that are contested by the insurance company. Lots of paperwork and less time in the hustle and bustle of the courtroom. But finally, he doesn't have to worry about the office rent and has a salary that allows him to breathe. He gets his own apartment and joins the popular Congressional Country Club.

On Saturdays, he heads for the links and signs up for a round or two. It's there that he's placed in a foursome with Charles Camalier Jr., who's on the governing board of the country club. Most everyone in Washington is familiar with Camalier & Buckley, the luxury leather goods and specialty gift business that Charles's family owns. Hogan & Hartson has even represented the Camaliers on real estate transactions.

"A single man?" Charles says, noticing that John doesn't have a ring on his left hand. "I ought to introduce you to my little sister."

"I'm pretty content as I am," John says.

"One dinner can't hurt. She needs to get out more. We'll consider it done."

When John picks up Lucy Camalier for dinner, he finds a petite woman, only five-foot-one. She's a graduate of the elite Maret School and the fashionable Fairmount Junior College. Lucy is shy, but underneath it, bubbling with personality. He learns that she has an exceptional singing voice—so good, in fact, that her operatic style won her admission to the acclaimed Julliard School of Music in New York, even though, in the end, her family felt New York City was too exotic for a young lady. She finds him knowledgeable about world affairs, and likes how he pores through the news the same way she does—although he's a good twenty years older than she is.

John clinks his glass against hers as dinner winds down. "I'd like to see you again, Lucy—though you should know, no matter what your brother told ya, I'm not the marrying kind."

Lucy moves her cloth napkin from her lap to the table, picks up her Camalier & Buckley bag, walks to the door, and hails a cab.

The next day, John sends flowers and chocolates with a note:

Dear Lucy,

I made a terrible mistake. Please accept my apologies. May we try again?

Yours sincerely,
John J. Sirica, Hogan & Hartson

~

The wedding announcement is published only five months later, in February 1952: "Mr. and Mrs. Charles Camalier Sr. announce that Lucy Camalier and John Sirica will wed at the end of February in Fort Lauderdale."

John writes Dempsey and asks him to serve as best man, confessing, *"I'm lucky to have such a wonderful girl after all the freedom I had."*

Dempsey obliges. At the wedding, he throws his arm around John's shoulder after the couple exchanges vows.

The year is a big one for other reasons, too. The presidential campaign promises to be robust, and John is gearing up for the next round of politicking. This may be the best opportunity for Republicans to regain the White House since 1932—the days when John worked in the U.S. attorney's office with Leo Rover.

The election brings fresh faces to the presidential campaign. On the Democratic side are Adlai Stevenson II, governor of Illinois, and John Jackson Sparkman, senator from Alabama. General Dwight D. Eisenhower heads the Republican ticket, paired with the thirty-nine-year-old senator from California, Richard M. Nixon, as his running mate. Nixon had come to public attention a few years earlier as a U.S. representative from Whittier, California, and a member of the House Un-American Activities Committee. Searching for Communist Party members who worked in the government, Nixon doggedly pursued Alger Hiss, a state department employee. When Hiss was convicted and sent to prison. Nixon's name emblazoned the headlines.

True to Frank Hogan's word, the law firm agrees to John's appearances on the campaign trail. Leonard Hall, Republican

National Committee Chair, sends John to Italian-American clubs in New Jersey, Connecticut, and Ohio.

Sporting a "Dick and Ike" button on his lapel, John gives pep talks: "We all know General Eisenhower is a hero who led the NATO forces in Europe. We need his sense of command and purpose. And Dick Nixon is a hardworking, seasoned member of Congress who will bring focus to the White House. As someone who sees up-close how Washington operates, I can tell you this is the team that we need."

When Eisenhower and Nixon sweep the election, Hall doesn't forget John's help. "I'm going to suggest you for the position of commissioner of immigration. As the son of an immigrant, you'll be the perfect candidate," he tells John over dinner one night.

John puts down his fork. "I'm glad that you're thinking of me. But I have my eye on the courts. The courtroom is like being inside the ring to me—every sense comes alive," he says. "I want to be considered for an opening on the trial bench."

"There aren't any openings on the bench," Hall says.

"If something opens up, that's when I want you to remember the name 'John J. Sirica.' I'm counting on you, Leonard."

Throughout Washington, the change to Republican leadership in 1953 unleashes a waterfall of activity. Not only is the White House in Republican hands, but so is the Senate.

John rushes home to tell Lucy that another opportunity has come his way. His friend, Joe McCarthy, now Senator Joe McCarthy, has called him. McCarthy is appointing a Permanent Subcommittee on Investigations in the U.S. Senate, which he intends to use to investigate Communist influence in the government. He needs a chief counsel, and who better than John?

Lucy listens quietly.

"This is really big, you know," John tells her.

"I don't think so," she says.

"Joe McCarthy is offering it to me. Me! Dempsey and I used to visit him in Wisconsin. He'd take us around to the local establishments and—"

"He can find someone else. You've got a good job at a firm—the best in town. After all those 'starvation years' in your own practice." She tugs at the flowing top she's wearing; it's only been a few days since she's needed maternity clothes. "We're building a new house in Spring Valley. We're going to have a family."

"It could be a stepping stone to a judicial appointment."

"It could be a disaster," Lucy replies.

"Chief counsel to a *Senate* committee. I would be one of a kind. I could run my own investigation."

"Why don't you think about it on your walk?"

She shoos him out the door for his daily five-mile exercise.

Joe McCarthy comes by their apartment later that night to talk about the position. Dempsey had always described McCarthy as a real "bar-room fighter"—and McCarthy accepted it as a compliment. "You bet," he'd say.

John doesn't buy into McCarthy's obsession with Communism. He had made a point of avoiding Red Scare politics in the FCC investigation and focused instead on corruption. But if he were in charge of McCarthy's investigation, he could find out if there was anything to the issue and steer it in the right direction.

The two sit at John's dining room table and McCarthy pulls out some notes. Before the senator can get going, John puts his palm flat on the table. His fingers are thick and hardened, a working man's fingers, now with a ring that makes a slight clink on the polished wood.

"I should let you know, Joe. The timing probably doesn't work for me."

"This is a big opportunity, John! This is a huge assignment. I've been trying to get this committee off the ground for years, and now I'm doing it."

"Lucy thinks it's too much to give up the firm . . . now that I've finally got a firm," John says. "Ya know me . . . all those lean years, scratching out a few dollars here and there. Finally, I have something steady. Top of the line. It's different than when Dempsey and I were pals selling war bonds. I was a bachelor then. Now I'm a family man, and coming to it late."

"But you'd be so good," McCarthy insists. "You can deliver a punch when you need to. Our Johnny! And the way you called out that FCC committee and that whitewash—first-rate. This subcommittee on investigations is going to be *big*—much bigger than the House Committee."

"It's a matter of circumstance, Joe. Ya understand, I'm sure."

McCarthy folds up his papers quickly. "If I can't convince you, I'm going with this New York fellow—Roy Cohn. That'll pipe down those people who say I'm an anti-Semite. This is going to be big!"

"Sure, Joe."

John doesn't bother to watch as the senator walks down the block. He closes the door and turns back inside.

Chapter Nine

A BLACK ROBE

The word flies through local legal circles in 1956: Judge Henry Schweinhaut of the Federal District Court for the District of Columbia—the court that handles major criminal and civil matters for D.C.—is resigning. This is one of the first D.C. openings since Eisenhower and the Republicans have taken the White House. Hats are being tossed in right and left by men who've waited for years for this opportunity.

"Federal judges can be independent and follow their conscience," John explains in a letter to Jack Dempsey. *"The founding fathers wrote that in the Constitution—and it's a wonderful thing."*

Dempsey writes back: *"I support you all the way, my friend! You will be a great judge."*

Judges to the Federal District Court for the District of Columbia are appointed by the president with advice and consent of the Senate. Called "Article III" judges because the process for naming them is set out in Article III of the Constitution, these are lifetime appointments.

Securing an appointment is political, and John knows that this is where the years of stumping for party candidates might finally pay off. He first tells the people on the Republican State Committee for the District about his intention to apply. Since he's serving on the committee, he's certain he'll have their support. But the chair for the Republican State Committee, George Hart, also has his eye on the position, and when the committee sends in its recommendation, Hart is the only name on the list.

Campaign manager Leonard Hall responds immediately and agrees to put in a good word for John at the White House. The District Bar Association, where John's been working on committees for years, submits his name on a recommendation list. John culls through business cards he picked up on the campaign trail. One man he met is working for the attorney general, and the attorney general reviews the recommendations for the president. John gets in touch.

The efforts pay off. John's nomination goes forward.

The final hurdle is a hearing before the Senate Judiciary Committee. Chairman James O. Eastland calls the hearing to order on March 19, 1957, at 3:05 p.m. in Room 327 of the Senate Office Building. John clenches his fists tightly for a moment.

The president of the D.C. Bar Association is first to speak. "Mr. Sirica has practiced law in the District of Columbia for over thirty years," he says. "We feel that he is extremely well suited—in fact, ideally suited—to be a judge of the United States District Court, both by virtue of his judicial temperament and his vast experience."

John himself is called next.

"Mr. Sirica, did you practice law by yourself?" Chairman Eastland asks.

John modulates his voice to his deepest register and wills

himself to speak calmly and confidently. "I started practicing around the courts—municipal court, police court. I practiced about three-and-a-half years, and was appointed by the then-United States attorney, Mr. Leo A. Rover, on August 1, 1930, to be assistant United States attorney for the District of Columbia. I remained in that position for approximately three-and-a-half years. I am now a member of the firm of Hogan & Hartson of the District."

"What type of cases did you try?" Eastland asks.

"I would say all types of cases—criminal, civil, radio cases. I am now specializing. Practically all of my time is devoted to trying negligence cases, on the defense side most of the time—at the firm."

George Hart, beaten out of the nomination, agrees to speak on John's behalf. He's angling for the next appointment.

"I think he is outstandingly capable. He has great integrity," Hart testifies.

And then it is done.

At 3:15 p.m., Eastland adjourns the committee. The nomination is approved.

Two weeks later, on April 2, 1957, the Ceremonial Courtroom on the sixth floor of the federal courthouse is lined with well-wishers for John's swearing-in ceremony: law luminaries, Lido Civic Club friends, Lucy, and a beaming Jack Dempsey. John holds one hand in the air, sturdy and firm, as he swears to uphold the Constitution of the United States of America.

Afterward, the chief judge takes John to the second floor of the courthouse. A nameplate is already affixed, and John runs his hand across it: Judge John J. Sirica.

He enters his office and surveys what will be his judicial home. Behind the door is a receptionist's area, and beyond that, a door to a spacious office for him, and another door into a separate room for a law clerk and a small library.

At one end, there is an entrance to the courtroom—*his* courtroom. John opens the door and climbs the three steps up to the judge's bench. The ceiling is thirty feet high and gives a sense of airiness, even auspiciousness, to the space. John looks out to where the defense gathers on one side and the prosecutors on the other—where he has sat dozens of times through cases of every sort.

Beyond the counsel tables from this view is the rail—really a waist-high wooden partition, with a swinging gate in the middle, that separates the court participants from the observers. Only lawyers, clients, witnesses, and court personnel are authorized to step in front of "the bar." Beyond the bar are the four rows of benches for spectators, all in the smooth, light wood that gives the room a contemporary feel befitting the opening of the new courthouse only a few years earlier. At the opposite end of the room are the heavy doors to the hallway of the courthouse, where witnesses and clients can gather. As the judge, he will be perfectly positioned to observe anyone who enters.

The chair for a witness is at his left hand—a small box raised just one step so that, as a judge, he can still look down on them. At the same height on the vertical wall to the left is the box for the jury. To enter and exit, they walk from the jury room on his left side and straight into the jury box. The floor in front of the bench has space for the court reporter to set up transcription equipment; the desk to the side is where the bailiff sits, and on the wall to the right, a place for marshals.

A flag stands on a pole to his side—he cannot help but walk past it every time he enters, and those watching the proceedings cannot help but see it framing him. Above his head, the wall behind him holds the round emblem of the court: a spread eagle with the words "United States District Court—District of Columbia."

John swivels the judge's chair in both directions. This feels right.

Boxes of books have been delivered to his chambers. He sifts through them and finds the binder with the hearings of the FCC Committee, and puts it on a shelf near his desk. He pulls out a picture of Lucy and their children. He organizes his desk neatly—pen in a holder, desk blotter, calendar with flip days— and when the maintenance staff comes by, he directs them to put up a portrait of William E. Leahy from the Teapot Dome case behind his desk. He wants lawyers to know that this is the gold standard he seeks in all who appear before him.

Almost immediately, a docket of cases is delivered. Each is different, unique, with its own set of facts and human dimension. People flow in and out of the courtroom, and there is always an electricity and excitement, even in the most mundane case.

The first case that goes to trial happens the day after the swearing-in ceremony, and John prepares carefully in advance, reviewing standard motions and organizing jury instructions into a three-ring notebook. He puts on his new robe with great care—Lucy had helped him measure and order it. The case is a charge of unauthorized use of a motor vehicle. He convenes the jury and listens intently through the half-day trial. The jury can't make up its mind, and the verdict—a mistrial—appears in a two-inch story in *The Star*. John clips it out anyhow: his name in the paper as "Federal Judge John J. Sirica." Only the second judge of Italian heritage to be appointed to the federal bench.

A lot of the learning happens on the job. Motions from the lawyers come fast—an objection to testimony, a request that a

charge be dismissed, a claim that the other side is asking leading questions, a demand that a witness be instructed to answer.
There's little room for hesitation. Sure, the judge can call for a
break in a trial and go research the matter, or ask a law clerk
to do so. But to do that on every motion and every objection
would stifle a trial or turn it into a ritual that never ends. Most
decisions are made on the spot, and Judge Sirica is good at that.
Allegations of error can end up as an appeal to a higher court,
but he doesn't fret about them. In the courtroom, he's in charge,
and he calls it as he sees it.

Now everyone calls him "Judge"—and not just in the
courthouse. At attorney gatherings, club events, parties, walks
through the neighborhood, even the parking lot: people greet
him simply as "Judge."

Within a couple of weeks, lawyers around the courthouse
are also taking the measure of the new judge. A man accused of a
$65 hold-up gets a four- to fourteen-year sentence. A man who
pleads guilty to the sale of narcotics gets a fifteen-year prison
sentence. The whispered nickname begins among the defense
lawyers and spreads quickly: "Maximum John."

"If you don't get a 'not guilty' verdict, watch out for the
sentencing. Sirica's a bear," the defense lawyers tell each other.

Lawyers learn more about Judge Sirica's habits. He's hardworking and expects attorneys to be the same. He doesn't take
kindly to nonsense from lawyers or clients. The judge is outspo-
ken in the courtroom. He'll question witnesses from the bench
if he thinks the lawyers aren't getting to the point or the client is
fibbing. He's especially irritable if he thinks someone is trying to
pull something over on him.

~

The cases mount over the years. Robbery, arson, bribery, extortion. In one, a man is charged with trying to rob a bus driver with a toy pistol, and in another, a man with a real gun robs a person at a bus stop. The judge gives a Teamster vice president a sentence of one year for contempt of Congress for refusing to testify, and does the same to a Ku Klux Klan wizard.

An antitrust case brought by a trucker against twenty-three railroad companies for claimed monopolistic behavior drags Sirica into a ten-month trial with one hundred lawyers and volumes of testimony, witnesses, motions. There is no time for a break and no days off. He writes to Dempsey: *"One of the things I would like to do is to play a lot of golf. I haven't been sleeping well for some time."*

In 1971, he takes on a high-profile murder that is setting the tabloids on edge. A man named Robert Ammitown reported that he and his wife were carjacked by a man who ordered them to a remote area and then raped and killed the wife. The police investigation uncovered a murder-for-hire plot by Ammitown, who pointed to a local pool shark as the murderer.

The alleged murderer is black, the husband is white—and both are implicated. When the prosecutors recommend a second-degree murder charge against the husband in exchange for his testimony against the alleged murderer, Judge Sirica rejects the plea agreement. It's not fair that the husband is being offered a lower charge, he says.

Later, Judge Sirica tries the case of the alleged murderer, and is further disturbed. He sends the jury out of the courtroom so he can question the man himself. It's an unusual move. He wants to know if the defendant used certain profane language when he reported to the husband that he had completed the contract.

When the defendant denies that he used such language, Judge Sirica scoffs.

"You'll never make me believe that story. You might fool this jury, but you can't fool me," he says.

The jury, as it happens, convicts.

There are pleasurable moments, too. He addresses law school graduates who are being admitted to the bar. He conducts marriage ceremonies on occasion—he poses with Jack Kent Cooke, owner of the Washington Redskins football team, and his wife, Jeannie, after they consecrate their marriage in his office.

Without a doubt, his favorite job takes place in the Ceremonial Courtroom on the sixth floor when the naturalization ceremonies for new Americans take place. In front of the group of men and women who have come from other places and other nations, with families surrounding them, he issues the oath of citizenship, and then speaks to them. At times like this, he hears echoes from his father.

Judge Sirica clears his throat:

"As new citizens, you have undertaken a responsibility and a commitment.

"We are blessed to live in a democracy. Our liberty is, and should always remain, the nearest and dearest thing to each and every one of us. This should be because it is upon our precious freedoms of choice, speech, press, religion, and action that our American way of life is based.

"You should be proud of your heritage, as I am as the son and grandson of immigrants. It is the combination and intertwining of so many great immigrant backgrounds, representing many nationalities, that have contributed so much to the growth and greatness of America. But also consider as new citizens that you have made a commitment to unite with your fellow Americans in order to achieve our nation's goals—including a desire to see that justice prevails. Justice is public and private; it is the habit or procedure of giving people that which is rightfully due to them.

"You have all heard, I am sure, that democracy is government by the people. The people must make it work. For this reason, I ask you to take your liberty to heart. That requires that we participate in those activities of government which affect our freedoms. That involves our being 'active' citizens. Each and every one of us can, and must, exercise our right to vote in every election, support vocally and monetarily the causes which we feel are right and just.

"We are founded on one of the world's greatest political documents. It reads as follows: 'We the people of the United States, in order to form a more perfect union, establish justice, ensure domestic tranquility, provide for the common defense, promote the general welfare, and secure the blessings of liberty to ourselves and our posterity, do ordain and establish this Constitution for the United States of America.'

"I hope you will cherish it as I do. Congratulations on becoming a citizen of the United States."

In 1971, Judge Sirica, after fourteen years on the bench, is the judge with the most seniority when the chief justice retires. By the rules of the District court, he automatically moves into the role of chief judge.

As the chief judge, he takes on a new responsibility: assigning cases.

Part Two

JUDGE JOHN J. SIRICA ENCOUNTERS WATERGATE

Chapter Ten

A SUMMER'S DAY IN 1972

Sundays afford Judge Sirica much-needed down time. He still rises at his regular 5 a.m., even at the age of 68 in 1972. The family's toy poodle, Coco, sleepily follows when the judge putters into his home office, where photos and memorabilia fill the walls.

In the summer, he and Lucy and the children—Jack, at nineteen, already in college; Tricia at fifteen; Eileen at nine—have breakfast together and then drive to the mid-morning Mass. In the afternoon, they might go out for a family lunch or head for a swim at the Congressional Country Club. The judge will manage to get in his daily walk, winding through the leafy northwest neighborhood where he and Lucy have built a comfortable home. Sometimes one of the children will tag along for some private time with Dad. In the evening, Lucy might commandeer the piano and do a sing-out of "Hello, Dolly!" or a favorite from *The Lawrence Welk Show*.

First thing in the morning, the judge sweeps up the

newspaper from the front yard where the delivery boy tosses it, and gives it a thorough read. In 1972, election news is everywhere again, and the judge regales in the details. President Nixon, up for his second term, is assured of the nomination at the convention in Miami Beach in August, although antiwar demonstrators are expected to create a ruckus. The Democrats, also convening in Miami Beach, are scheduled for July, and have a horse race on their hands with leading contender Senator George McGovern vying for the ballot along with a host of others: prior frontrunner Edmund Muskie of Maine, former Vice President Hubert Humphrey, Governor George Wallace of Alabama, Senator Henry Jackson of Washington, and U.S. Representative Shirley Chisholm of New York.

The still-ongoing war in Vietnam is foremost in people's minds. Passions are stirred by the Pentagon Papers, leaked by Daniel Ellsberg a year earlier. The massive document is a secret government study of the war, criticizing U.S. involvement and describing clandestine war activities and the undisclosed bombing of Cambodia. Nixon, while furious about the leak, adopts "Peace with Honor" as his campaign slogan. He tries to focus on accomplishments—opening a door to China; becoming the first U.S. president to visit Moscow; establishing the Environmental Protection Agency. Nixon claims to speak for a "silent majority" and continues the "law and order" promises of his 1968 campaign. Judge Sirica is particularly fond of this tough-on-crime approach.

On a lazy Sunday, June 18, 1972, the front page of the *Washington Post* immediately grabs the judge's attention: "5 Held in Plot to Bug Democrats' Office Here."

The byline is that of police reporter Alfred E. Lewis, who is familiar to the judge since he handles so many of the District's crime cases. But unusually, another eight writers are listed as contributing to the story. Two are new names to him: Carl Bernstein and Bob Woodward.

The judge starts reading the story while walking back into the house, then reads it standing inside the front door, and then again, sitting down on the couch in his office.

Sunday, June 18, 1972. Washington D.C.

Five men, one of whom said he is a former employee of the Central Intelligence Agency, were arrested at 2:30 a.m. yesterday, June 17, in what authorities described as an elaborate plot to bug the offices of the Democratic National Committee here.

Three of the men were native-born Cubans and another was said to have trained Cuban exiles for guerrilla activity after the 1961 Bay of Pigs invasion.

They were surprised at gunpoint by three plain-clothes officers of the metropolitan police department in a sixth floor office at the plush Watergate, 2600 Virginia Ave. NW, where the Democratic National Committee occupies the entire floor.

There was no immediate explanation as to why the five suspects would want to bug the Democratic National Committee offices or whether or not they were working for any other individuals or organizations.

All wearing rubber surgical gloves, the five suspects were

captured inside a small office within the committee's head-quarters suite.

Police said the men had with them at least two sophisti-cated devices capable of picking up and transmitting all talk, including telephone conversations. In addition, police found lock-picks and door jimmies, almost $2,300 in cash, most of it in $100 bills with the serial numbers in sequence.

The men also had with them one walkie-talkie, a short wave receiver that could pick up police calls, 40 rolls of unex-posed film, two 35-millimeter cameras and three pen-sized tear gas guns.

The story goes on to explain that a twenty-four-year-old African-American security guard by the name of Frank Wills had noticed something amiss during his rounds. Finding a piece of tape on a stairwell door to prevent it from locking, he removed it. When he made a repeat visit to the stairwell a short while later, a new piece of tape was on the door latch. He immedi-ately called the police. The police found the sixth-floor entrance jimmied open; the entire floor held the offices—twenty-nine of them—of the Democratic National Committee.

As they worked their way through the space, guns drawn, the police called out. Hiding behind a screen, five men volun-tarily stepped forward when the police came close. They were arrested and taken to the second-district police headquarters for booking. All of the men gave false names and presented fake identification. Four defendants were from Miami. Their real names were Bernard L. Barker, Frank A. Sturgis, Virgilio Gonza-lez, and Eugenio R. Martinez.

In a thirty-minute arraignment before Superior Court Judge James A. Belson, the four Miami men refused to cooperate, except to say they are "anti-Communists." They had connections to anti-Castro organizations. The fifth man, James W. McCord Jr., told the court that he was a security consultant who had recently worked for the government. When pressed about what branch of government, he quietly said, "CIA." This detail was particularly intriguing to the reporters who were covering the court.

At the arraignment, Assistant U.S. Attorney Earl J. Silbert urged Judge Belson to order the five men held without bond. Silbert called the men professionals with a "clandestine" purpose. Judge Belson decided to release the men on bond.

Even for Washington, D.C., where politics rises like the heat in summer, this story is out of the ordinary.

By the time Judge Sirica drives to the courthouse the next morning, more information fills out the picture.

Washington Post reporters Bob Woodward and Carl Bernstein have a new story. James W. McCord not only has CIA connections, but is also a former FBI officer and is employed as the Chief of Security by the Republican Committee to Re-Elect the President (CRP). The CRP—Nixon's official campaign organization with offices at 1701 Pennsylvania Avenue NW— is headed by former Attorney General John Mitchell, a close friend of the president. Mitchell immediately issues a statement saying that McCord was a one-time security contractor for the Republican Committee, but is no longer on the payroll.

"McCord is the proprietor of a private security agency who was employed by our committee months ago to assist with the installation of our security system. We wish to emphasize that this man and the other people involved were not operating either in our behalf or with our consent," says Mitchell. But when reporters get their hands on the payroll listings, McCord's name is there.

The case grows stranger and stranger.

The prosecuting attorney, Earl Silbert, collects a trove of information in possession of the five defendants. Some of it was on them when they were arrested; other items are discovered after search warrants are issued for two hotel rooms they rented at the Watergate Hotel. There are address books, checks, another $4,200 in cash in sequentially numbered $100 bills, and more bugging equipment.

White House Press Secretary Ronald Ziegler immediately dismisses any White House connection. "I'm not going to comment from the White House on a third-rate burglary attempt," he says.

On June 22, five days after the men are arrested, President Nixon speaks to the issue publicly for the first time. "The White House has had no involvement whatever in this particular incident," he says at a press conference.

Additional names surface. One is E. Howard Hunt, Jr. His name is found on papers held by the suspected burglars. A White House phone number is next to his name. Hunt is a former CIA officer, a novelist with more than forty books to his name, and most recently, a consultant in the White House, working with political operative Charles Colson, who has the title of Special Counsel to President Nixon.

In July, the New York newspaper *Newsday* reports that the FBI has been trying to interview G. Gordon Liddy about the Watergate affair. A former aide in the Nixon White House, Liddy moved to the Committee to Re-elect the President as counsel to its fundraising arm. He's been an FBI agent and a prosecutor in Duchess County, New York, who was once reprimanded for shooting a gun at the ceiling inside a courtroom. In D.C., his penchant for carrying a holster with a gun under his suit jacket earns him the nickname of "Cowboy on the Potomac."

On August 1, the *Washington Post* that lands on Judge Sirica's lawn carries another blockbuster story. The headline says "Bug Suspect Got Campaign Funds." Judge Sirica immediately takes note. A money trail. This story traces a $25,000 cashier's check deposited to the account of one of the arrested men. The check was signed by a donor to the Committee to Re-elect the President. It had been delivered to Maurice Stans, Nixon's chief fundraiser and former Secretary of Commerce, and then deposited in the account of Bernard Barker, one of those arrested at the Watergate. On the same day, an even larger sum—$89,000 in four checks from a Mexican lawyer—had been deposited in Barker's account. Barker's account also turns out to be the source of the $100 bills with sequential serial numbers confiscated from the five suspects.

Over the summer, prosecutor Silbert convenes a federal grand jury to hear testimony. Among those called to testify is Alfred Baldwin, a former FBI agent who was stationed at a Howard Johnson's motel across the street from the Watergate to act as a lookout for the burglars during the break-in. Jeb Stuart Magruder, Deputy Campaign Director for CRP, is questioned about payouts and job assignments.

President Nixon makes another statement on the Watergate caper on August 30. He declares that White House Counsel John Dean has conducted an investigation of the matter and that no one from the White House was involved in it.

On September 15, the grand jury returns indictments against seven men—the five caught in the act of burglary at

Democratic headquarters in the Watergate building, as well as Liddy, who is said to have managed the operations, and Hunt, a co-manager who recruited the Miami team. There are eight counts. Counts 1 and 2 are for conspiracy. Counts 3, 4, 5, and 8 are about the electronic surveillance. Counts 6 and 7 apply to McCord and the Miami men and relate to the possession of electronic surveillance equipment.

The *Washington Post* points out that the indictments seem limited, failing to address "central questions about the purpose or sponsorship of the alleged espionage." The indictments don't even mention the $25,000 check from the Republican donor or the $89,000 from the Mexican lawyer.

Now that indictments have been issued, there's a new challenge for Judge Sirica—he must assign the case to a trial judge. On September 18, he announces his decision about who will be the presiding judge on the case: he will do it himself.

Judge Sirica sets a trial date for November 15. That's after the presidential election on November 7, but he doesn't see how it can be ready for trial any earlier.

"The case simply can't be forced into some electoral time frame," the judge tells his clerk, Todd. "I know there are critics out there who want it to happen right away, but the prosecution has the right to collect its evidence and the defendants have the right to a fair trial. That's the way the system works, election or not."

In the meantime, the *Washington Post* continues to run explosive stories. John Mitchell, who mysteriously resigned as Campaign Chair in July, operated a secret slush fund while serving as attorney general to pay for Republican "information and intelligence" operations to undermine Democrats. Other high-level names are surfacing including the Treasurer and other officials of the Republican Committee to Re-Elect the President.

A long article in the *Washington Post* on October 10 takes the story to another level. The Watergate break-in, it reports, is part of a "massive campaign of political spying and sabotage conducted on behalf of President Nixon's re-election and directed by officials of the White House and the Committee to Re-elect the President." As many as fifty people are involved in trying to sow confusion and disinformation inside the Democratic Party with a variety of "dirty tricks." One is a letter published in a newspaper in Maine that derails the candidacy of Sen. Edward Muskie, accusing him of making derogatory comments about locals of Canadian descent. The letter was a complete fabrication of the "dirty tricks" team, according to the reporters, but the accusations stick. The names of a political operative who engaged in spying on Democrats and a deputy director of communications in the White House enter the mix.

Other than the *Washington Post*, most of the media ignore Watergate. There's an article here and there in the *New York Times* or the *Los Angeles Times*, but surveys show that fully one-half of the American people are not even aware of the Watergate matter. More attention is on the back and forth of the presidential election: Who's saying what? Who is up or down in the polls?

The results of the November 7 presidential election are clear immediately. "Nixon Wins in Landslide" says an early headline in *The Philadelphia Inquirer* that stretches across all eight columns of the front page. Forty-nine states go for Nixon—the only places that the electorate goes for McGovern are Massachusetts and the District of Columbia. President Nixon has a smashing victory: 60.7 percent of the popular vote, and 520 of

538 Electoral College votes. For the first time, the majority of Italian Americans swing to the Republican side.

"Now that the election is over, it is time to get on with the great tasks that lie before us," President Nixon says in a speech to the nation from the Oval Office. "I tried to conduct myself in a way that would not divide our country, not divide it regionally or by parties, or in any other way. I very firmly believe that what unites America today is infinitely more important than those things which divide us."

The editorial writers at the *Washington Post* are more skeptical. "Did most voters know of the excesses and improprieties and even alleged illegalities in his campaign?" they ask. "We do not concede that Tuesday's vote has closed the books on these accounts."

After all, the trial of the alleged burglars is still to come. The date for the trial has now been moved to January because Judge Sirica's doctors warn him that prolonged sitting will exacerbate a pinched nerve in his back. Even so, the judge is able to listen to preliminary matters—what items will be introduced as evidence, what witnesses will be called, what information the prosecution must share with the defense.

It's in December that Judge Sirica gets a better idea about how prosecutor Silbert plans to approach the case. Going through pre-trial evidentiary reviews, Silbert is talking about bugging equipment and tools, but doesn't mention anything about the money that has been found in the hands of the defendants or how it got there.

The judge is curious. The newspaper accounts are impossible to miss—they have not only been front-page news, but also included in motions before the court.

"Are you going to offer any evidence on the question of how

the $25,000 check got into the possession of Mr. Barker?" the judge asks Silbert, flipping through papers.

Silbert hesitates for a moment. "The check hasn't yet been entered into the pre-marked exhibits."

"Are you going to try and trace—I think there is an item of $89,000?" Judge Sirica asks.

Silbert shifts his weight from one leg to the other. "A key witness may not be available."

"Now on the question of motive and intent in this case, as you know there has been a lot of talk about who hired whom to go into this place. Is the government going to offer any evidence on the question of motive and intent for entering the Democratic National Committee headquarters?"

Silbert looks at the file folders on the table in front of him and mutters that the jury will be able to draw inferences.

Judge Sirica drops both hands on the bench with a loud thump. He doesn't care if he seems intimidating. "This is going to be one of the crucial issues in the case—why did they go in there? Who hired them, if somebody did hire them?"

Back in his chambers, the judge looks up when Todd knocks on the door. Judge Sirica likes his pleasant manner, serious research, and inquisitive nature. He's a clean-cut fellow, a graduate of Brigham Young University and Duke University School of Law.

"Your Honor, do you want me to catalog any of the evidence?" Todd asks.

"I know I was a bit hard on Silbert." The judge rolls up his shirtsleeves. "I wanted to make the point, directly to him. We need to get to the truth of this matter."

"It does seem that the jury will want to know about motivation."

"It's not just that these men were paid, but *why* were they paid? What was behind it?" The judge swivels to his bookshelf. "I'm going to give this to Silbert!" He holds the blue bound book of the FCC hearings high in the air.

"Your Honor?"

The judge thrusts the volume in his direction, and Todd wraps his whole hand around the edges.

"This may be thirty years old, but the tricks are the same," Judge Sirica explains. "This is how a whitewash is engineered. I'll tell you one thing I know for sure: I'm not having it in my courtroom. Go where the evidence takes you. Let the chips fall where they may."

"A whitewash? With seven defendants . . . and all of their lawyers? That would take a lot of maneuvering, wouldn't it, Your Honor?"

"I don't know what's going on, Todd, but this doesn't smell right and it doesn't look right. Frankly, it doesn't feel right in the gut. I don't care how high it goes. That's why we have an independent judiciary. The public has a right to know, and I intend to safeguard that."

Chapter Eleven

A BURGLARY TRIAL

The trial begins, finally, on January 10, 1973.

After months of preparation, motions are settled. Sixty witnesses are listed. Jurors are selected—eight female and four male residents of D.C. are seated. Criminal Case No. 1827-72 begins.

Judge Sirica calls upon Earl Silbert to deliver the opening statement for the prosecution. Here is Silbert's opportunity to outline what he plans to show. The best prosecutors create a compelling narrative, a storyline that the jury can watch unfold over the course of the trial.

Silbert says that the prosecution will describe a covert operation conducted by Gordon Liddy and Howard Hunt that began early in the campaign. The Committee to Re-Elect the President had delivered $235,000 in $100 bills to Liddy for intelligence operations. There had been, he explains, a prior eavesdropping operation at the Watergate Democratic Headquarters in May. Albert Baldwin, across the street at the Howard

Johnson's, had been monitoring the conversations picked up by the electronic bugs and typing up transcripts, but the sound was poor and a second entry was needed. Silbert describes $100 bills being passed out to participants before the break-in, and how, after the first five were arrested, Liddy raced back to the offices of the CRP and started shredding papers. There, he encountered a fellow staffer and proclaimed: "The boys got caught last night. I made a mistake. I'll probably lose my job."

For the five men arrested at the scene, this was a case of financial gain, Silbert says. The four Miami team members were experiencing hard times and were in it for the money. James McCord's consulting business was on the skids. The other two were the organizers. Howard Hunt was responsible for recruiting the Miami men.

"Gordon Liddy is the boss," Silbert adds.

Judge Sirica, listening, fiddles with his gavel handle and glances at the jury. That's one of the things he learned as a young lawyer from Bert Emerson—keep an eye on the jury.

To hear the prosecutor's narrative, Liddy was a rogue employee and the buck stopped with him. He was supposed to undertake legitimate intelligence gathering, but he operated outside the bounds of his assignment and the Watergate break-in was the result. Silbert mentions no higher-ups.

The judge surveys the courtroom. Defendant Liddy, dressed in a natty suit, smiles throughout the prosecutor's opening statement and even laughs from time to time. At one point, he seems to wave to the jury as if he's the star on a TV show.

From the bench, the judge catches a view of the flag that sits to his right. This very courtroom is the one where citizenship ceremonies are held, ceremonies during which he points to the flag as a symbol of the United States and the U.S. Constitution.

A muscle spasm curls around the nerve in his back. As Silbert finishes his two-hour monologue, the judge calls a recess. In chambers, he lies on a couch to rest his back.

The pinched nerve is what had forced him to postpone the trial date from November in the first place. His back had seized up without warning in October when he and Lucy attended a judge's conference in New Orleans. They always looked forward to the annual gathering of judges from around the country, the camaraderie of equals from disparate locations, dealing with similar issues and concerns. Seminars would discuss a variety of topics—court security, hiring practices, rules of ethics, new transcribing equipment, educational programs for school children. In the evenings, the judges and spouses would share a meal and talk into the night. This year, he and Lucy joined a group at a linen-covered table in the French Quarter on Saturday evening, with handshakes all around.

As the dinner chatter turned to the upcoming Nixon-McGovern election, Judge Sirica suddenly felt intense pain shoot down his spine and leg. Like a boxer who gets knocked hard on the chin, he didn't let on how much it hurt, but on the way back to the hotel, he could barely hobble along on Lucy's arm.

"Compressed nerve. A touch of sciatica. Too much sitting, too much stress," the doctor told him when he returned to D.C. "Hot compresses, cold compresses. Slow down. Vary your routine. Self-care, we call it. If you're not careful, you could face permanent damage."

The judge moves forward the trial date for the Watergate caper. Days, the judge stands at his desk; evenings, Lucy gives him gentle massages on the lounger in his home office. The healing is slow but steady.

Now, with the short respite from the bench, the sharp

discomfort begins to recede. While on break from opening statements, he calls Todd over.

"Make sure you have handy the rules of criminal procedure that allow a judge to question a witness directly," Judge Sirica tells him. "I know the prosecutors get their feathers all ruffled and the defense lawyers try to make points out of it for appeal, but it's my job to get to the truth, and I'm not going to rule it out."

After lunch, the defense attorneys begin their opening statements. The lawyer for James McCord says that McCord had no *intention* of committing a crime at all.

"He had no evil-meaning mind. He had no evil-meaning hands," the lawyer declares with a dramatic flair.

Without meeting the "intent" requirement—the *mens rea*—McCord can't be guilty, his lawyer says. But he doesn't offer an alternative explanation of why on earth his client would be in the Democratic headquarters of the Watergate building with bugging equipment at 2:30 a.m. Judge Sirica scribbles a note.

Next, the lawyer for the Miami men speaks. He argues that his clients acted with patriotism in mind, and without knowing the big picture.

"The evidence will show," he says, "that the men were following instructions that they have been trained to follow, with no evil motive." They were, he says, merely following orders.

This time, Judge Sirica interrupts. "Is it your defense that they were taking orders from somebody—that they were ordered to go into the Watergate?"

The Miami men at the defense table shift uncomfortably in their seats. The lawyer answers with vague pronouncements about the temple of justice and so on, until Judge Sirica interrupts again.

"The jury is going to want to know why the men went in there," he says. "Who paid them? Did they get any money to go in there? Was it purely for political espionage? What was the purpose?"

The attorney for Howard Hunt, when his turn comes, asks to approach the bench. After listening for a moment, the judge instructs the marshal to lead the jury out. As soon as they have departed, Hunt's lawyer announces that his client wishes to plead guilty to three charges that have to do with burglary and conspiring to conduct surveillance. The prosecutor acknowledges that he accepts these terms.

Hunt sits blankly at the defense table. He is looking gaunt, and his lawyer mentions that he has lost fourteen pounds in the past month. Only weeks earlier, Hunt's wife, carrying thousands in $100 bills, had been killed in a plane crash, leaving Hunt and four children, ages nine to twenty-two.

Judge Sirica is well aware of what a guilty plea will mean: no testimony from Hunt, an apparent ringleader. With no testimony, there is no opportunity to get the whole story, whatever it is. The truth will fall silently by the wayside.

"It is the practice of this court," the judge speaks crisply to the lawyer, "to send defendants to jail after they enter a guilty plea—whether it is a white-collar crime or a crime of violence." He looks over at Hunt and back at his lawyer. "You ought to have that in mind; Mr. Hunt ought to have that in mind."

Since it is now late in the afternoon, the judge says that he will further consider Hunt's plea overnight. A judge is not obligated to accept a plea simply because the defense lawyer and prosecutor agree on it. That's what he'd done with the husband who hired a contract killer to murder his wife—rejected his plea, even though the prosecutor had accepted it.

"What do you think of Hunt's plea?" the judge asks Todd when they are back in the chambers. His law clerk is really the only person with whom he can discuss the case under ethics guidelines.

"He's been working for the CIA for decades, according to the pre-trial report. All over the world."

"Yes. He's well educated. Has connections to the White House."

"The pre-trial report notes he'd requested a postponement after his wife was killed."

"Yes, yes, a tragedy. We can all agree that's a tragedy," the judge replies. "But I think he's going silent for some other reason. This is stonewalling. Someone is buying his silence."

When court resumes the next day, Judge Sirica takes up Hunt's plea agreement again. "The government has a very strong case against Mr. Hunt," he says to Hunt's lawyer. "For this reason, I am refusing to accept a plea to only three of the charges. If Mr. Hunt wants to plead guilty, he will have to plead guilty to all six charges against him. The public interest in justice allows no less."

Hunt's lawyer pops up. "Mr. Hunt pleads guilty to all six charges."

"Do you understand the consequences of pleading guilty?" The judge directs his question directly to Hunt.

"Yes, Your Honor, I do." Hunt is on his feet now, too.

"Very well. I would like you to describe more of the events surrounding the break-in at the Watergate."

"I have nothing to add, Your Honor." Hunt is immobile, hands at his side.

Seeing that he is getting nowhere, the judge sets the bail bond at $100,000. Three hours later, Hunt posts the bond and is out again. As Hunt heads home, he stops to speak to waiting reporters.

"Anything I may have done, I did for what I believed to be in the best interest of my country," he says.

"Are higher-ups implicated? Is there a broader conspiracy?" one of the reporters calls out.

"To my personal knowledge, there was not," Hunt says, fixing his fedora and turning to walk in the opposite direction.

That leaves six defendants in the courtroom.

When the session resumes, it's prosecutor Silbert's turn to approach the bench.

"Your Honor, I have a letter from some of the defendants." He hands the document up to the judge.

After a quick read, Judge Sirica tells the marshal to bring the four Miami men, their lawyer, and the prosecutors back to his chambers.

"Mr. Barker, is this your letter?" he asks as the men take seats.

"Yes, Your Honor," says Barker.

"And the rest of you know the contents of this letter and agree?"

Sturgis, Martinez, and Gonzales all nod.

The letter is to their lawyer, Henry Rothblatt: "We have been asking you since Sunday, January 7, 1973, to change our plea from 'not guilty' to 'guilty.' We have made it clear from the beginning that the defense you presented in opening statements and to the press is not acceptable to us."

Judge Sirica puts the letter on his desk, face down. "Mr. Rothblatt?"

"I do not agree with that position. I refuse to enter guilty pleas for these men."

Now the judge turns back to the four men. "Since your counselor has indicated that he cannot accept your position, do you wish to have a new lawyer?"

"Yes, Your Honor," they answer in unison.

"Do you wish for me to appoint a new lawyer?"

"Yes, Your Honor."

By Monday morning, a new veteran lawyer is at the defense table in the courtroom with the four men.

"My clients," he says, "wish to change their plea."

"In a moment," the judge responds. "First, I wish to read a letter signed by Mr. Bernard Barker into the record."

His mind wanders for a second. Who had taught him that? Along the way, over the course of forty-six years in the law, he has made it his habit: Get it on the record. Still, this one makes his temple throb. Over the weekend, a credible article in the *New York Times* has reported that the four are being pressured to plead guilty and are being offered hush money to prevent them from saying anything. If that's what is happening, the truth about Watergate is sinking further into the grave, right before his eyes.

Judge Sirica reads the letter out loud, making sure the court reporter hears each word, and then calls the four men before the bench. Even without the jury in the courtroom, they stand stiffly, military style.

"I want you to be straightforward with these questions. I want you to come forward in a truthful manner," he tells them. They nod.

Judge Sirica asks them if they understand the charges and the sentences they might face—standard questions. Together and separately, they answer, "Yes."

"Are you giving this plea freely, knowing that you might be sentenced to fifty-five years in prison?"

"Yes," the men answer.

"Are you being paid by anybody for anything?" the judge asks.

"No," the men say, all in one voice.

The judge repeats the questions that have been bothering him from the outset, reeling them off, one after the other.

"For what purpose did you four men go into the Democratic headquarters? Who, if anyone, hired you to go in there? Are there other people—that is, higher-ups in the Republican Party or the Democratic Party or any party—involved in this case? What was the motive? Who was the money man? Who did the paying off?"

He turns to Martinez. "I want you to start from the beginning and tell me how you got into the conspiracy. I don't care who the answers might help or hurt. Don't pull any punches."

Martinez answers: "I believe the facts that you have read in the charges are true."

"That's a blanket statement," the judge replies. "Who recruited you for this operation?"

"Maybe I offered myself," Martinez says. His body is unflinching.

"Who paid you?"

"I did not get paid, Your Honor, for my services, except for expense money," Martinez says. "Money doesn't mean a thing to us, Your Honor. I own a hospital in Cuba, one of the best hospitals. I own a factory of furniture in Cuba. I was the owner of a hotel in Cuba. I left everything in the hands of the Communists there. I lost everything so money, really, is not a great deal in my decisions."

"What were you talking about in your room before the break-in?" the judge asks, drawing upon his best trial interrogation technique: Do not ask a yes-or-no question, do not lead the witness, do not ask vague questions. Seek a specific answer to a specific question.

"I want to forget all the things. I don't want to remember anymore," Martinez says.

"Have you ever done work for the CIA?" the judge asks.

"Not that I know of," Martinez replies.

The judge looks over as defendant Liddy slaps his knee and laughs.

The other two answer similarly. They are not in it for the money; they don't know the purpose of the break-in, but they were told it would help their Cuban cause; they know of no one else who is involved.

Now, the judge turns his attention to Barker, who seems to be the leader of the four. Perhaps he can be convinced to answer.

"Why was Mr. Howard Hunt's number at the White House in your address book?" the judge asks.

"I have had the privilege of knowing Mr. Hunt for a long time," Barker replies, his hands clasped behind his back.

"Were you working under the direction of Mr. Hunt or other people in this job that you pulled off?" the judge asks.

"I was working with Mr. Hunt. I was completely identified with Mr. Hunt. I had the greatest honor. I worked with him as my superior. I have known what my responsibilities are and I will face all my responsibilities," Barker says.

"Who, then, sent you the $114,000 that was deposited in your account?"

"For a definite fact, I can't say who sent that money," Barker says.

Judge Sirica shakes his head. The amounts of money are

astounding: a regular car like the Ford Galaxie 500 is selling for $3,880, so the figure is the equivalent of nearly thirty cars.

"Didn't it seem rather strange that you would receive $114,000 and not know where it came from?"

"I don't think it is strange, Your Honor. I have previously before this been involved in other operations which took the strangeness out of that as far as I was concerned."

"These $100 bills that were floating around like coupons . . . where did they come from?"

"I assume it was in connection with the operation of the Watergate," says Barker. "I got that money in the mail in a blank envelope."

The judge looks down at him from the bench. "Well, I'm sorry, I don't believe you."

He accepts their guilty pleas, places them on $100,000 bond, and the marshal takes them away to the jail.

The judge looks at the defense table. Now there are two: Gordon Liddy, the "boss," and James McCord, the electronic eavesdropping expert who supplied most of the equipment.

The lawyer for McCord moves for a mistrial because, he argues, the jury will see that five defendants are missing and will naturally conclude that they have pled guilty. This will prejudice the rights of his client, he says.

"Motion denied." Judge Sirica speaks firmly.

"Your Honor, I believe that is an error that I will be forced to raise on appeal."

The lawyer is not a regular in D.C., so the judge adds a coda. "I'm not awed by the appellate courts. Let's get that straight. All they can do is reverse me. They can't tell me how to try a case in my courtroom."

Over lunch, he sits with Todd in chambers and throws his hands in the air. "Five of the seven defendants off the trial. None of them 'know' anything," he says.

"It does seem that it will make the case harder," Todd says.

"The 'chips can't fall where they may' if there are no chips in evidence."

"Is there anything the court can do?" Todd uses "the court" like casebooks do—to refer to what is really Judge Sirica.

"I know that I'm not required to sit there like a nincompoop while they try to pull the wool over the eyes of the court," Judge Sirica replies, brushing some crumbs off his shirt.

Back in the courtroom, the actual testimony finally begins. The prosecutor calls his witnesses to the stand. First is a college student who was recruited to spy on the Democratic campaign. Next, the security guard at the Watergate testifies, and then the police officers who came upon the burglars. Detectives testify about their investigative work—tracking down names in address books.

Alfred Baldwin is the eighteenth witness. He testifies that he was hired in May by James McCord to monitor the phone lines with electronic bugs on them from a second-floor hotel room at Howard Johnson's across from the Watergate, and then to type up transcripts. Both Liddy and Hunt inspected the setup, he says.

The original bugs were placed in late May, but weren't producing good results. Baldwin transcribed 200 calls, and once a day, McCord would come by to pick up the logs. One time, Baldwin testifies, McCord asked him to write the name of a particular person on a package and deliver the transcript himself to the Committee to Re-elect the President. He says he cannot remember the name that he had put on the envelope.

As the court recesses for the weekend, Judge Sirica hangs his robe in chambers.

"The lawyers are not developing all the facts," he remarks to Todd, slipping on his overcoat.

His clerk nods sympathetically.

"It's ironic," the judge continues. "All this going on at the courthouse about the campaign, and tomorrow's the inauguration."

"My wife and I are planning to watch the parade down Pennsylvania Avenue—it's a first for us," says Todd. "There's a theme of 'Spirit of '76'—coming up to the 200th anniversary this term." He slings his coat over his shoulder and walks to the door with the judge.

"I'll sit this parade out at home," Judge Sirica says. "I have plenty to think about with this Baldwin fellow. He's been given immunity in exchange for testimony, but he seems to have forgotten an awful lot of critical information."

On Monday, Baldwin resumes his testimony.

Under cross examination, the lawyer for McCord seeks to elicit from Baldwin that he thought the operation was legitimately connected to security issues. He doesn't ask about higher-ups.

Judge Sirica pulls off his glasses and asks the marshal to lead the jury out.

"I have some questions for Mr. Baldwin. All of the facts have not been developed. This is perfectly proper and is not accusing anybody of any wrongdoing by asking these questions," the judge says.

He turns to the witness. "You stated that you received a telephone call from Mr. McCord from Miami, in which, I think, the substance of your testimony was that he wanted you to put one particular log in a manila envelope, and he gave you the name of the party to whom the materials were to be delivered, correct?"

"Yes, Your Honor."

"You wrote the name of that party, correct?"

"Yes, I did."

"What is the name of that party?"

Baldwin, still seated in the witness chair looks sideways in Judge Sirica's direction. "I do not know, Your Honor."

"When did you have a lapse of memory as to the name of that party?" the judge asks.

Baldwin sits mute.

"Here you are, a former FBI agent—you knew this log was very important?"

"That is correct," Baldwin replies.

"Yet you want the jury to believe that you gave it to a guard, is that your testimony?"

Again, Baldwin is mute.

Judge Sirica slaps shut a notebook in front of him and dismisses Baldwin from the stand, while signaling the marshal to bring the jurors back.

Next in the witness chair is Jeb Stuart Magruder, who, as Deputy Campaign Director, is second in command at the Committee to Re-elect the President. He is the highest-ranking official from the CRP to testify. In his command at the CRP were 250 full-time employees and 25 division heads. He says that he gave Liddy assignments to gather political intelligence and to create an "intelligence network," but he knew nothing of illegal activities.

"I emphasized that the acts of our committee would be

handled in a legal and ethical manner," Magruder testifies. He never told Liddy to bug the Democratic headquarters, he says.

At the bench, Judge Sirica dashes words onto a legal pad and underlines them, some more than once. "Who knew? Who authorized?" He pauses for a moment, considering the case. *These witnesses are trying to deliver one line of thought: No one knows anything. Liddy did it all on his own, they seem to say. Liddy, meanwhile, sleeps at the defense table most of the time, and when he isn't sleeping, he sneers at the bench or waves to the jury like a joker, mocking the proceedings.*

The treasurer of the CRP testifies next. He states that he paid Liddy $199,000, adding that mere hours after the arrests, he saw Liddy in the hallway at the CRP. Liddy told him that he made "a mistake"—his "boys" got caught and that he had used someone from the committee, which he said he would never do.

Judge Sirica breaks in again and asks the marshal to lead the jury out. He snaps the treasurer with questions.

In response, the treasurer repeats the story about encountering Liddy in the hallway, but adds a new phrase: Liddy tells him that he used someone from the committee "which I told them I would never do." To the judge's ear, the phrase "I told them" implies that other people—higher-ups—are involved.

"What was the purpose of turning $199,000 over to Liddy?" the judge asks the treasurer.

"I have no idea," the witness says.

"You have no idea?"

"No, sir."

"You can't give us any information at all?"

"No, sir. I was merely authorized to distribute the money. I was not told the purpose."

The judge holds his hand open. "You didn't question the purpose of the $199,000?"

"No, sir. I verified with Mr. Stans and Mr. Mitchell that he was authorized to make those."

"You verified it with who?"

"Secretary Stans, the finance chairman, and—I didn't directly, but he verified it with John Mitchell, the campaign chairman."

"Didn't anybody indicate to you by their action or words or deeds what this money was to be used for?" The judge stares at the treasurer.

"No, sir."

The judge announces to the parties that he intends to read the treasurer's answers back to the jury. The lawyers jump up with objections. The prosecutor offers to re-question the treasurer in front of the jury.

"No," Judge Sirica replies. "He might have a lapse of memory."

The defense attorneys object, too. Judge Sirica is unruffled.

"I am concerned with doing what I think is the right thing at the moment," he tells them.

As soon as the marshal brings the jury in, the judge reads the back-and-forth with the treasurer.

The prosecution completes presenting its witnesses—fifty-one in all—on the fifteenth day of the trial, January 29, 1973.

The lawyers for McCord and Liddy wrap up the entire defense case in two hours. Each presents three witnesses who testify that the defendants have excellent reputations. Neither Liddy nor McCord takes the stand.

At last come the closing arguments. Prosecutor Silbert zeroes in on a meeting at a local hotel, attended by all seven of the men originally charged.

"And there you have the classic conspiracy. All the conspirators together, plotting, planning, conspiring together," he says. "Gordon Liddy is the mastermind, the boss, the money-man. Yes, he had been authorized to carry out intelligence activities for the Committee to Re-elect the President. But he was not content to follow out what he was supposed to do. He had to twist it, to divert it. Liddy and McCord went off on an enterprise of their own."

He ends with a flair. "When people cannot get together for political purposes without fear that their premises will be burglarized, their conversations bugged, their phones tapped . . . you breed distrust, you breed suspicion, you lose confidence, faith and credibility. Bring in a verdict that will help restore the faith in the democratic system that has been so damaged by the conduct of these two defendants and their co-conspirators."

Given his chance, the lawyer for McCord argues again that his client had no criminal intent.

"He is loyal to his country," the lawyer says.

Judge Sirica interrupts. "You are only giving your personal opinion."

Liddy's attorney says that his client actually had no hand in the Watergate caper. While Liddy headed an intelligence unit for the Committee to Re-elect the President, Watergate was carried out by others, and Liddy was betrayed by his friend Howard Hunt.

After instructions from the judge, the jury retires to deliberate. One hour and thirty-eight minutes later, the jury returns with its verdict. Judge Sirica tells the two defendants to rise and the deputy court clerk reads the verdict out loud.

G. Gordon Liddy is found guilty on all counts: conspiring to burglarize, wiretap, and eavesdrop; burglarizing with the intent to steal property; burglarizing with the intent to wiretap; endeavoring to eavesdrop illegally; endeavoring to wiretap illegally; and illegal wiretapping. James W. McCord is guilty on all those counts and two more: possession of wiretapping equipment and possession of eavesdropping equipment. Sentences on all of the counts, combined, could run from thirty-five to fifty-five years.

Judge Sirica accepts the verdict. He never doubted the outcome—the evidence is overwhelming—but he's not happy. The truth behind the break-in is still unknown.

"I am not satisfied that all the pertinent facts that might be available—I say might be available—have been produced before an American jury," he says at the bond hearing for Liddy and McCord. "Everyone knows that there is going to be a congressional investigation in this case. I would frankly hope—not only as a judge, but as a citizen of a great country and one of millions of Americans who are looking for certain answers—I would hope that the Senate committee is granted the power by Congress to try to get to the bottom of what happened in this case. I hope so."

He sets the sentencing for March 23, 1973. Gordon Liddy waves as the marshals march him away.

"Don't worry," the judge says to Todd in chambers. "It's not the end."

Chapter Twelve

A LETTER TO THE JUDGE

One night in February, unable to sleep, Judge Sirica gets up at 3 a.m. Coco barely lifts an eye to see him moving toward his desk.

"One thing they should know," he tells Coco. "I am not a damn fool."

The judge starts flipping through the federal code. A judge in another jurisdiction has mentioned "conditional sentencing" or "provisional sentencing," and the judge is certain he once used it in a narcotics case. Provisional sentencing would allow him to give a temporary sentence and then review it later, in the meantime putting the defendants on notice that he will take into consideration what cooperation they provide.

"That might break out some truth," he tells Coco.

If he makes this part of his sentencing approach, perhaps the defendants will give answers in court or before the Senate committee now looking into the Watergate incident. Since the end of the trial, Congress, the media, and the public have all taken a deep interest in Watergate.

The Monday after the trial ended, Senator Sam Ervin had introduced a resolution to fund a committee to investigate the Watergate affair, officially known as the Senate Select Committee on Presidential Campaign Activities. One thing it will need: witnesses who will talk honestly. The prosecutors, prodded by Judge Sirica, have also indicated that the grand jury will continue to look at Watergate.

Of course, tough sentences are nothing new in Judge Sirica's court, and that reputation might come in handy in this case. Harsh sentencing fits his reputation as "Maximum John." He's hard on convicted criminals, no doubt about it, but he's the same across the board. White-collar criminals get the same treatment as everyone else; in fact, the judge thinks that people who have the advantage of a college education and a position of responsibility bear a special burden when it comes to following the law. President Nixon may have used "law and order" as a campaign slogan, but Judge Sirica lives it every day.

The judge puts a plan in motion. In every case, the probation department completes a pre-sentencing report on convicted criminals. The judge decides to send special questions to the probation officer who will be interviewing the burglary trial defendants. He wants the probation officer to ask "Who sent the burglars into Watergate?" "What was the motivation?" "What was the intention?"

Back in his second-floor chambers at the courthouse, Judge Sirica has his secretary type up the questions and asks part-time law clerk Richard Azzaro to deliver them to the probation department—it's in the same building, so it's merely a stroll down the hallway.

Probation officer James D. Morgan runs through Sirica's questions and begins asking them of each Watergate defendant. When James McCord comes in, he's dressed in a jacket and tie as usual. He's prepared to answer questions about his career, his family, his disabled daughter who needs special care, his two other children, his church activities, his community work.

Morgan opens his folder. "I have some questions which may go toward mitigating circumstances that the judge will take into consideration: Can you tell me who sent you into the Democratic headquarters in the Watergate? What was the intention?"

McCord can feel his temperature rising. If he refuses to answer, he'll be labeled as uncooperative. If the answers contradict what eventually comes out in the Senate hearings, they might be used against him to bring other charges. He's not eager to go to prison, but he holds his tongue.

On March 20—just three days now before the sentencing hearing—McCord visits the federal courthouse and heads up to Judge Sirica's chambers.

As a part-timer, Richard is stationed alone in the judge's reception area when McCord enters. McCord nods and drops his briefcase on a table. He clicks open the latch and pulls out a sealed letter.

"I have a letter I want to deliver to Judge Sirica. Personally," he tells Richard.

The clerk looks surprised. In his short tenure in the office, he's not seen a defendant in the judge's chambers—not anyone who's just popped in. As far as he knows, defendants are not supposed to come to the judge's chambers without their lawyers present. But the courthouse rules are still new to him.

"Let me check," he says, trying to remember if Todd is in

the clerk's room or the library upstairs. Surely he will know what to do.

Before he can move, Judge Sirica opens the door to the reception area, straightening his tie and slipping on his sports jacket to head to lunch in the judge's dining room. He takes one look at McCord and closes the door as quickly as he opened it. He buzzes his secretary on the phone.

"Mrs. Holley, please tell Richard to come in here immediately," he says.

When the clerk enters, the judge motions for him to close the door tightly.

"You know that's James McCord? Watergate?"

"Yes, sir."

"What is he doing here? Why are you talking to him?" the judge says, standing rigidly with one fist on his desk. "He's not allowed to come to my chambers."

"He says that he has a letter he wants to deliver to you. Personally. I wasn't sure what to—"

"Tell him to leave. Now. I will NOT take a letter from him. I will not take anything from him. If he has a letter, he can give it to James Morgan in the probation office. Or to his attorney. They can deliver it. I WILL NOT take anything directly from him."

"Yes, sir. I'll tell him."

After McCord leaves, the judge calls Todd and Richard into his office.

"You be careful! McCord coming in here? I'm not getting caught in any trap," he says. "Suppose he put money in the envelope? Suppose he's trying to set me up? I've prosecuted gamblers and crooks—defended them, too—and I know they have a bag of tricks as big as a truck. A former CIA man? We're going to take this step-by-step through the proper procedure, everything documented. We'll see where it goes."

Later that day, probation officer James Morgan comes to the judge's chambers. He has McCord's letter, still sealed. The judge tells Morgan to sit, and he calls in Todd and Richard and his court reporter. He wants witnesses to see what's in the envelope. Once all are assembled, he carefully opens the envelope and there it is: only a letter—nothing else. Two pages, single-spaced.

Then the judge gets his first glance at what it says.

Certain questions have been posed to me from Your Honor through the Probation Officer, dealing with details of the case, motivations, intent, mitigating circumstances. In endeavoring to respond to these questions I am whipsawed in a variety of legalities.

Several members of my family have expressed fear for my life if I disclose knowledge of the facts in this matter either publicly or to any government representatives. Whereas I do not share their concerns to the same degree, nevertheless, I do believe retaliatory measures will be taken against me, my family, and my friends should I disclose such facts. Such retaliation could destroy careers, income, and the reputations of persons who are innocent of any guilt whatsoever.

In the interest of justice and in the interest of restoring faith in the criminal justice system which faith had been severely damaged in this case, I will state the following to you at this time which I hope may be of help in meting out justice in this case.

Upon reading further, the judge realizes this is a crack in the stone wall that has been hiding the truth about Watergate.

McCord's letter continues:

1. There was political pressure applied to the defendants to plead guilty and remain silent.

2. Perjury occurred during the trial of matters highly material to the very structure, orientation, and impact of the Government's case, and to the motivation of and intent of the defendants.

3. Others involved in the Watergate operation were not identified during the trial, when they could have been by those testifying.

It goes on:

I would appreciate the opportunity to talk with you privately in chambers. Since I cannot feel confident in talking with an FBI agent, in testifying before a grand jury whose U.S. Attorneys work for the Department of Justice, or in talking with other government representatives, such a discussion with you would be of assistance to me.

The letter ends:

I give the statement freely and voluntarily, fully realizing that I may be prosecuted for giving a false statement to a judicial officer. The statements are true and correct to the best of my knowledge and belief.

Judge Sirica takes off his glasses and places them on the desk. He sits quietly for a moment, as do the others. He rubs one eyebrow.

"This," the judge begins, "is a very important letter. Very. All of you here are the only people inside the courthouse who know about this letter. You must pledge to say nothing until we address it in the proper forum."

The two clerks, the probation officer, and the court transcriber all nod in agreement.

As the staff members exit the room, Judge Sirica waves Todd back in. "Close the door."

After it clicks, the judge picks up the letter again and waves it in the air. "This is it. This is what I have been waiting for."

"You believed someone might be convinced to open up," Todd says.

"And that someone is James W. McCord, Jr. This could break the matter wide open. Some T.R.U.T.H." The judge massages his neck. "Now we have to decide what to do with it."

"Get it on the record. Isn't that what you always say?"

"Yes, exactly. And so we will," the judge replies. "The sentencing hearing is only a few days away. There is a lot on the docket already, what with the seven men, and the dispositions that I plan to present. But I will do this first. That will be the best time."

～

On Friday, March 23, the judge puts on his glasses immediately after he takes his place on the bench.

"I have something to put on the record in this matter before we enter the disposition phase," he announces to the courtroom. "I have in hand a letter that is addressed to me and was delivered to the probation officer. I will now read it for the record."

As soon as the judge finishes, a dozen reporters jump up and race for telephones in the corridor. While McCord's information has clues, it names no one in particular. But Samuel Dash, newly named chief counsel of the Senate Watergate Committee, is observing in the courtroom when the judge reads the letter. He knows exactly what—and how much—this letter means to a Senate investigation that has hit wall after wall.

Judge Sirica leaves the courtroom briefly after reading McCord's letter. He looks for a glass of water and drops into his chair. After all of the angst and worry about the possible twisting of justice in the trial, he's feeling the toll.

In twenty minutes, he returns to hand out sentences.

He begins with the four Miami men and Howard Hunt. "None of you has been willing to give the government or other appropriate authorities any substantial help in trying this case or in investigating the activities which were the subject of this case," he says.

He announces maximum terms under the law: forty years each to the Miami men—Barker, Sturgis, Martinez, and Gonzalez—plus a fine of $40,000; thirty-five years plus a fine of $40,000 to Hunt. He emphasizes that these are "provisional sentences" and will be reviewed in three months.

"I recommend your full cooperation with the grand jury and the Senate Select Committee. You must understand that I hold out no promises or hopes of any kind to you in this matter, but I do say that should you decide to speak freely, I would weigh that factor in appraising what sentence will be finally imposed. Other factors will, of course, be considered, but I mention this one because it is one over which you have control. I sincerely hope that each of you will take full advantage of any such opportunity."

In truth, he knows that eventually the conspirators will get lower sentences, four or five years, and after that, they can petition for reductions. But the message is loud and clear: more cooperation, a better sentencing outcome.

Judge Sirica adds: "Some good can come from a revelation of sinister conduct whenever and wherever such conduct exists. I am convinced that the greatest benefit that can come from this prosecution will be its impact in spurring corrective action so these activities will not be repeated in our nation."

In light of his letter, McCord's sentencing is postponed for the time being.

That leaves Gordon Liddy. Throughout the trial, Liddy has been wearing his involvement in criminality like a badge of pride. Even today, Liddy greeted spectators upon entering the courtroom with his goofy wave.

His lawyer urges the judge to consider the whole of his history. "Mr. Liddy's life has been one of public service. It has been deeply involved with the law."

"Does the defendant have anything to say?" Judge Sirica asks.

"I have nothing to say, Your Honor." Liddy stands stiffly. "Nothing to say."

The judge looks down at him, standing on the floor below

the bench. He notices Liddy has lost some weight in the federal penitentiary in Danbury, Connecticut, where he's been incarcerated since the trial. Liddy is a lawyer, a former assistant district attorney, a former FBI special agent, and a former White House aide—a well-educated man with experience in law and politics.

"The knowing and deliberate violation of laws deserves a greater condemnation than a simple careless or uncomprehending violation," the judge says. "The crimes are sordid, despicable, and thoroughly reprehensible."

Judge Sirica announces that he is skipping the provisional review. Liddy has shown nothing but disdain throughout the proceedings. The judge instead delivers the final sentence: Liddy is ordered to serve a minimum of six years and eight months in prison, up to a maximum of twenty years, with a $40,000 fine.

"This sentence is meant to be a deterrent to others," the judge says.

Liddy doesn't flinch. The guards move him out of the courtroom for the transfer back to prison.

Although the judge doesn't know what the actual machinations in Watergate are, he feels that McCord's letter has finally pulled back a curtain. But even he can't predict the bombshell that awaits in the Senate.

Chapter Thirteen

AN UNRAVELING

Two days after the judge releases McCord's letter, Watergate Senate Counsel Samuel Dash calls a press conference. A criminal law professor at Georgetown University and a former prosecutor in Philadelphia, Dash is now serving as the lawyer to the Senate committee headed by Senator Sam Ervin. He says that he has spent the weekend interviewing James McCord, and that McCord has "named names." McCord will testify at public hearings.

The *Los Angeles Times* quickly fills in the gap on those names: Jeb Stuart Magruder, deputy director of the Committee to Re-Elect the President, who had denied any knowledge of Watergate events in Judge Sirica's courtroom; and John Dean, White House Counsel, the most direct connection to the administration so far. The trouble is that most of McCord's information is secondhand—he's gotten it from Liddy, and Liddy isn't talking.

John Dean, a preppy thirty-four-year-old with a boyish

face, has served as the White House Counsel since July 1970. He previously served as associate deputy to Attorney General John Mitchell, with whom he is friendly, and in various other short-term positions since his graduation from Georgetown Law School in 1965. In the White House, Dean reports to, and takes assignments from, John Ehrlichman and Bob Haldeman, Nixon's top advisers.

Dean's name has barely surfaced in the Watergate matter so far. Nixon had mentioned him in late August 1972, when he assured the nation that his White House Counsel had conducted an investigation of the Watergate incident and cleared the White House. Dean's name also came up in late February 1973 when Acting FBI Director L. Patrick Gray testified to Congress. Asked about Watergate, Gray said that he had given reports on FBI activities to Dean and also received documents for destruction from him. The mention of Dean makes an impression when McCord brings it up.

All soon understand that there is more to Dean's story than they had imagined—he has a vast knowledge of activities inside the inner sanctum, both before and after the Watergate burglary. Dean gets a lawyer and starts talking to Watergate prosecutor Earl Silbert in early April and, separately, to Sam Dash at the Senate committee. He implicates, along with himself, a telephone directory of participants in planning or covering up Watergate: Haldeman, Ehrlichman, Mitchell, Magruder—and President Nixon, too.

Separately, Magruder also begins to meet with the prosecutors. He now offers a different version of events than he gave in Judge Sirica's courtroom. He describes meetings well before the Watergate incident with Liddy, Mitchell, and Dean to establish a budget for intelligence operations that included wiretapping and break-ins. On April 12, his lawyers strike a deal with the prosecutors, agreeing that he will plead guilty to a single felony of conspiracy to obstruct justice, defraud the United States, and wiretap the Democratic headquarters.

Now, it seems, every magazine, television station, and newspaper is covering the Watergate caper. Judge Sirica and Todd go through a stack of papers and magazines during their lunch hour.

A story in *Time* magazine describes a unit in the White House that, prior to Watergate, has wiretapped reporters and others—it's called the "Plumber's Unit" and it's run by Gordon Liddy, Howard Hunt, and Charles Colson. The *Associated Press* writes that Hunt and Liddy ran an operation out of the White House in 1971 to break into the offices of Daniel Ellsberg's psychiatrist to get dirt on the Pentagon Papers leaker. The *Washington Post* ties John Mitchell and John Dean to payments to silence the burglars and says $350,000 funneled to the conspirators came directly from a safe in the White House. The *New York Times* reports the grand jury is looking into a Watergate cover-up.

A revised picture is emerging of what was happening behind the White House curtains. Among the most disturbing: hush money to pay off the defendants and negotiations about executive clemency in exchange for silence.

Judge Sirica is watching TV in his study at home with Lucy on April 30, 1973, when President Nixon gives a major address. Everyone in the country seems to be watching TV that night.

"I want to talk to you tonight from my heart," Nixon says. "There has been an effort to conceal the facts both from the public—from you—and from me. It was the system that has brought the facts to light, a system that in this case has included a determined grand jury; honest prosecutors; a courageous judge, John Sirica; and a vigorous free press."

The judge glances at Lucy as he tries to absorb the president's injection of his name into this speech.

The president continues. "In any organization, the man at the top must bear the responsibility. That responsibility, therefore, belongs here in this office. I accept it." He then proceeds to announce a massive personnel sweep. He is accepting the resignation of Bob Haldeman. He accepts the resignation of John Ehrlichman. Attorney General Richard Kleindienst is leaving, too, because of close ties with people implicated in the Watergate investigations. And John Dean has been let go.

"There can be no whitewash at the White House," the president says.

Judge Sirica quietly repeats the word "whitewash" that became so important to him at the FCC hearings.

The president announces that he is nominating Secretary of Defense Elliot Richardson for the position of attorney general and that he will have "absolute authority" over the Watergate investigation. Later, in confirmation hearings, the Senate presses Richardson to name an independent counsel on Watergate, and he agrees. Shortly after he takes office, Richardson designates law professor Archibald Cox, a former solicitor general, to take over the Watergate case from Earl Silbert.

As a result, two tracks of investigation are underway. Cox, the new special prosecutor, under the rules in place at the time, works in private with the grand jury and can bring criminal charges for conspiracy or obstruction of justice. The Senate committee with Senator Sam Ervin as the chair and Sam Dash as the chief counsel can take public testimony and propose remedial legislation.

The prospect of public hearings by the Senate committee is generating so much attention that all three syndicated networks put their soap operas on hiatus to provide all-day coverage, and radio networks have wall-to-wall hearings, too; PBS will rebroadcast at night. Cameras fill the Senate Caucus Room, Room 318 of the Old Senate Office Building, for the opening of the hearings.

Senator Ervin guides the Senate Watergate inquiry with a folksy, storytelling manner, but underneath it all, he is a serious constitutional scholar. A Democrat from North Carolina with a grandfatherly voice, Ervin takes his place at the front of the hearing room, joined on each side by three Democrats and three Republicans.

"We are beginning these hearings today in an atmosphere of the utmost gravity. The questions that have been raised in the wake of the June 17 break-in last year strike at the very under-girding of our democracy. What they were seeking to steal was not the jewels, money, or other property of American citizens, but something much more valuable—their precious heritage, the right to vote in a free election.

"It has been alleged that, following the Watergate break-in, there has been a massive attempt to cover up all the improper activities, extending even so far as to pay off potential witnesses and, in particular, the seven defendants in the Watergate trial in exchange for their promise to remain silent—activities which, if true, represent interference in the integrity of the prosecutorial and judicial processes of this nation."

Low-level functionaries at the Committee to Re-Elect the President testify first. Then the Senate committee turns to the police officers who conducted the arrests, then McCord, the Miami men, and people who worked on the Republican

Committee—the committee treasurer, the finance chairman, and others.

"I never imagined so many people were involved," Todd says to the judge as they listen to a radio broadcast in the office.

"They're working their way up," Judge Sirica observes. "We'll see how high it goes."

Only a week into the Senate hearings, on May 22, President Nixon releases a new statement about Watergate, changing what he has said previously. The *Washington Post* calls the 4,000-word statement "extraordinary."

"I had no prior knowledge of the Watergate bugging operation," the president writes. "People, without my knowledge or approval, undertook illegal activities in the political campaign of 1972.

"With hindsight, it is apparent that I should have given more heed to the warning signals I received along the way about a Watergate cover-up. It is clear that unethical, as well as illegal, activities took place in the course of that campaign. To the extent that I may in any way have contributed to the climate in which they took place, I did not intend to; to the extent that I failed to prevent them, I should have been more vigilant."

The president's new statement, now admitting that illegal activities have occurred, prompts Special Prosecutor Cox to visit Judge Sirica in his office.

"There is so much attention to the Senate hearings, Your Honor, that I fear it's going to make it impossible to prosecute the offenders. The media is everywhere. It's making the job of the grand jury increasingly difficult, and if we have to go to trial, we may never be able to find an impartial jury."

Judge Sirica nods in agreement. "I understand your concern."

"You have the power to protect a future prosecution. You can order the Senate to stop the hearings," Cox says.

"No, I can't agree to that, counselor." The judge pauses. He knows it's not what Cox wants to hear. "Stopping the hearings will lead the public to think there's a plot to hide the truth. Public confidence in our system is paramount. We are strong enough to withstand Senate hearings, and some good might come out of it. Let the chips fall where they may."

On June 15, the Senate committee calls Jeb Stuart Magruder as a witness, and Judge Sirica can't help but notice how much his testimony has changed. All sorts of things that eluded him in court are now in his recollection.

But it's John Dean whom everyone is waiting to hear. His testimony is scheduled to begin on June 25.

Sitting in a leather chair in his home office, Judge Sirica sketches out some of the known events of Watergate.

In the White House, Gordon Liddy and Howard Hunt were part of "the Plumbers," the unit set up to undertake covert intelligence operations and funded by cash held in private safes. When the Committee to Re-Elect the President gets going in 1972, Liddy moves to a position there. In March 1972, Campaign Chair John Mitchell in a meeting with John Dean and Jeb Magruder grants Liddy a budget of $250,000 for intelligence operations.

The first attempt to place electronic bugs in the Democratic Headquarters at the Watergate is on May 26, 1972, but the wiretaps turn out to be useless. The same cast of characters returns on June 17, 1972, to redo the bugs. The arrests happen then.

After the arrests, a different layer of activity begins behind the scenes. A full "containment" policy is pressed. Liddy begins destroying documents, even shredding cash. McCord buries and destroys equipment. Magruder burns files about other covert activities. Hunt's safe, entrusted to Dean, is cleared and the contents dumped. Some files are placed in the hands of Acting FBI Director Patrick Gray; others are simply thrown into the river.

Only four days after the break-in, as money held by the burglars is traced to campaign funds, increased containment efforts are made. The FBI and the Justice Department are pressed to report to the White House on their activities. Throughout, the president denies any involvement.

Hush money is collected to secure the defendants' silence. Bundles of cash are left for the burglary defendants in brown envelopes in telephone booths, airport lockers, and other places by a former New York City police officer hired for that purpose. Hundreds of thousands of dollars are transferred to the defendants from a secret campaign fund, but the demands continue. Hunt becomes increasingly agitated as payments lag; McCord will not agree to the payment amounts.

Judge Sirica reviews his notes and sighs. There's so much here, but so much more to know.

The real question at the Senate hearings comes from Republican Senator Howard Baker of Tennessee: "What did the president know and when did he know it?" He asks it of every witness.

So on June 25, when John Dean is called to testify before the Senate committee, he is ready to answer. It's now five months since the end of the trial in Judge Sirica's courtroom.

Dean wears horn-rimmed tortoise shell glasses that give him a youthful but studious look.

"Certainly, it is a very difficult thing for me to testify about other people. It is far more easy to explain my own involvement in this matter, the fact that I was involved in obstructing justice, the fact that I assisted another in perjured testimony, than to talk about what others did," he says.

He then launches into a 245-page statement that he reads in a dull monotone over the course of six hours. It's accompanied by forty-seven documents of handwritten notes and White House memos. Chronologically organized, the statement is fortified with extensive recitations of dates and details of his and others' involvement in setting up and then covering up Watergate.

Judge Sirica sees startling red flags. He is not alone. "Incredible stories," writes *Washington Post* reporter William Greider.

Dean tells of meetings with Haldeman, Ehrlichman, and former attorney general John Mitchell. But his toughest shots hit squarely at the president.

The cover-up began, he says, once the White House realized that James McCord was among the original five arrested, since he was on the staff of the Committee to Re-Elect the President.

Dean became "a conduit" for information and action. Haldeman and Ehrlichman told him what to do and he conveyed that to the campaign staff, the men who'd been arrested, and government officials. He met with Gordon Liddy. He cleared out Howard Hunt's safe. He met with the FBI director, and then set up regular communications with Henry Peterson, the prosecutor who had supervisory authority over Earl Silbert. Dean arranged for money to be raised to pay off the burglars and for other money to be transferred from a secret cash fund in the White House to someone who would distribute it. He learned that Charles Colson was seeking executive clemency for Howard

Hunt and he tried to facilitate the same for McCord. He prepared people inside the White House for grand jury testimony, some with falsified statements.

On the day that the indictments against the burglars came out, September 15, Dean spoke directly about Watergate with the president for the first time. The president congratulated him for stopping any prosecutorial action beyond Liddy.

"I left the meeting with the impression that the president was well aware of what had been going on regarding the success of keeping the White House out of the Watergate scandal, and I also had expressed to him my concern that I was not confident that the cover-up could be maintained indefinitely," Dean testifies.

In February 1973, the president told Dean to report to him directly on Watergate rather than through Haldeman and Ehrlichman. Dean says that he again told President Nixon that he did not think the Watergate matter could be contained.

Dean says that he continued to have direct meetings with the president—twenty-four meetings, fourteen phone calls. On March 13, he discussed payoffs and executive clemency for the men convicted in Judge Sirica's courtroom.

"I told the president that there were money demands being made by the seven convicted defendants. And that the sentencing of these individuals was not far off. He asked me how much it would cost. I told him that I could only make an estimate that it might be as high as a million dollars or more. He told me that that was no problem."

Dean says that he presented a thorough report directly to President Nixon on March 21, 1973. "I began by telling the president that there was a cancer growing on the presidency, and that if the cancer was not removed, that the president himself would be killed by it." Dean goes through the names of people in the White House or campaign who had received wiretapped information, and describes cash payments from the White House to the burglars. "I then proceeded to tell him that perjury had been committed, and for this cover-up to continue, it would require more perjury and more money. I told the president that I did not believe that all of the seven defendants would maintain their silence forever; in fact, I thought that one or more would very likely break rank.

"I thought it was time for surgery on the cancer itself and that all those involved must stand up and account for themselves," Dean reports. But that afternoon, in a meeting with the president, Haldeman, and Ehrlichman, he instead saw more plotting.

Judge Sirica takes particular interest in Dean's discussion of the events of March 23. According to Dean, a colleague called mid-morning to tell him about McCord's letter and that Judge Sirica read it in open court. Dean, in turn, called Ehrlichman. "After my conversation with Ehrlichman, the president called. Referring to our meeting on March 21 and McCord's letter, he said: 'Well, John, you were right in your prediction.'"

Dean continues with his chronology, detail after detail. On April 15, Dean says, the president asked to meet. The president's demeanor in this meeting was different. "The president, almost from the outset, began asking me a number of leading questions, which made think that the conversation was being taped," he says. President Nixon says that he was only "joking" when he said that $1 million in payoff monies would not be a problem. At one point, the president slides over to a corner of the room and whispers that it might have been foolish to have discussed executive clemency.

For four more days, the Senate committee grills Dean. Judge Sirica listens closely, as if he were imagining Dean in his courtroom. Senators look for contradictions, big and small. One senator asks about money that Dean removed from a safe for personal use. Another senator runs through a series of questions supplied by the White House: Dean doesn't waver. The judge is well aware, of course, that people who have committed crimes—and Dean has admitted them—may have motivation to stretch the truth. Dean might be doing just that.

Senator Lowell Weicker of Connecticut reads off a list of "proven or admitted" crimes committed by the executive branch: conspiracy to obstruct justice, conspiracy to intercept wire or oral communications, subornation of perjury, conspiracy to obstruct a criminal investigation, conspiracy to destroy evidence, conspiracy to file false sworn statements, conspiracy to commit breaking and entering, conspiracy to commit burglary, misprision of a felony, filing of false sworn statements, perjury, breaking and entering, burglary, interception of wire and oral communications, and obstruction of criminal investigation.

Senator Ervin adds to the list the potential violation of the constitutional duty of the president under Article II of the Constitution "to take care that the laws are faithfully executed."

President Nixon speaks out again, denying involvement once more. He reinforces the statement he issued on May 22: He did not know about the burglary in advance; he knows nothing about offers of clemency or efforts to provide the defendants with funds; he did not participate in any effort to cover it up.

The White House version of the discussions in various meetings is completely the opposite of Dean's version. About the March 21 meeting in which Dean says there is a "cancer on the presidency" and mentions the payoff money, the president says that he told Dean "that it was wrong, that it would not work, that the truth would come out anyway."

Time magazine writes, "Dean's motives remained suspect since he obviously hoped to avoid a long prison term for his admitted illegal acts. Dean's direct charges against the president still lacked corroboration."

Dean's testimony seems like it will hang in the air indefinitely—it is essentially his word against the word of the President of the United States.

Until July 16.

On July 16, Alexander P. Butterfield, former deputy assistant to the president and a former top aide to Bob Haldeman, takes the oath before the Senate Watergate Committee. Butterfield had been responsible for day-to-day operations in the presidential quarters. Following up on John Dean's notion that he was being taped, the committee asks a single question.

"Mr. Butterfield, are you aware of any listening devices in the Oval Office of the president?" a committee lawyer asks.

Butterfield takes a deep breath. "I was aware of listening devices, yes, sir."

This piece of information sizzles through the hearing room and grabs the attention of listeners across the country: The president's conversations were being taped.

Butterfield describes a complete sound-activated taping system, concealed in small holes drilled in the wood of the president's desk, installed in light fixtures and on the telephones. Other systems are in the Executive Office Building, the Lincoln

Room, and the cabinet room. The president secretly tapes all of his conversations, Butterfield says, a fact known only by a handful of people.

If Dean's sensational descriptions of conversations with the president are accurate, the tapes will bear it out. If Dean's statements are false, as the president says, the tapes will tell. One way or the other, there can be independent proof about what the president knew and when he knew it.

The Senate Watergate Committee and Special Prosecutor Cox separately agree: they need the tapes to complete their investigations.

Chapter Fourteen

THE TAPES

U sually most of Washington shifts from its business self to a more leisurely tourist mode in the summer. The busy corridors of the courthouse empty out; few cases are scheduled as judges and lawyers go on vacation. Judge Sirica normally would head for the beaches at Rehoboth Beach in Delaware with his family.

As of July 16, 1973, the Capital City is anything but normal.

With Butterfield's testimony, the Senate committee immediately asks the White House to turn over the tapes. So does Special Prosecutor Cox for use in the grand jury investigation. The president declines both.

On July 24, Special Prosecutor Cox brings a document to Judge Sirica—a subpoena.

The *subpoena duces tecum* demands that the president turn over eight tapes made on six specific dates: June 20, 1972, three days after the burglary when Nixon, Haldeman, and Ehrlichman met; June 20, 1972: a telephone conversation between Nixon and John Mitchell; September 15, 1972: the president's discussion with Dean on the day that the seven burglars were indicted; March 13, 1973: a conversation between Dean and the president; March 21, 1973: the report where Dean says that there is a "cancer" on the presidency; March 21, 1973, a discussion of Haldeman, Nixon, and Dean on hush money and clemency; March 22, 1973, a meeting by White House operatives with John Mitchell about how to move forward on Watergate; April 15, 1973, the conversation between Nixon and Dean where Dean feels that he is being taped.

The judge carefully reads the document. "Not many subpoenas for the White House come through here," Judge Sirica comments without even a touch of humor in his voice.

"My research indicates this may only be the second time in history," says Cox. "Justice Marshall did issue a subpoena against President Thomas Jefferson in the matter of Aaron Burr. Burr, you may recall from your days in law school, was being tried for treason."

Judge Sirica looks up. Cox, known for his bow-tied appearance, is a revered constitutional scholar and one of the country's experts on executive privilege. But the judge's law school studies are four decades in the past, and he has no recollection of any professor mentioning executive privilege.

"In any case," the judge says, "this subpoena makes perfect sense. Every prosecutor needs to have highest and best evidence to take to the grand jury. That's undeniably true."

The judge signs the order.

Young lawyers on Cox's staff serve the subpoena at the White House. At the same time, the Senate Watergate Committee is attempting to subpoena tapes separately, using its congressional powers.

Two days later, on July 26, Todd raps on the door of the judge's office, even though the door is open. He slips in and closes the door behind him.

"There's an attorney named Douglas Parker from the White House. He says he has something to deliver to you, and he wants to give it to you in person." Todd holds out Parker's card.

Judge Sirica inspects the seal on the card. "Send him in."

Todd returns with a young man, who hands the judge an envelope.

The judge reads the contents and quickly turns to Todd. "Get everyone to the courtroom—special prosecutor, grand jurors, get them all here."

Parker adjusts his suit jacket around his shoulders. "Your Honor . . . ." He's mentally scanning the rules of procedure, not quite sure what protocol is being deployed—he's only been sent to deliver the letter.

"I'm going to read it in open court," Judge Sirica says.

"Now?" says Parker.

"Yes, now. We're putting this on the record. Right now."

When Cox and the members of the grand jury are assembled in the courtroom, the judge takes the bench and holds up the envelope.

"I received a letter about twenty minutes ago from this fellow here—Douglas Parker. He's an attorney with the White House. I will now read you what the letter says."

The judge glances down to make sure the court reporter is ready, then reads aloud.

"Dear Judge Sirica:

"White House counsel have received on my behalf a subpoena

duces tecum issued out of the United States District Court at the request of Archibald Cox. The subpoena calls on me to produce for a grand jury certain tape recordings as well as certain specified documents. With utmost respect for the court of which you are Chief Judge, I must decline to obey the command of that subpoena. In doing so, I follow the example of a long line of my predecessors as President of the United States who have consistently adhered to the position that the president is not subject to compulsory process from the courts.

"I have concluded that . . . it would be inconsistent with the public interest and with the constitutional position of the presidency to make available recordings of meetings and telephone conversations in which I am a participant and I must respectively decline to do so.

"Sincerely,
"Richard M. Nixon."

There is a moment of quiet in the courtroom. No one inhales, and a slightly confounded "Now what?" expression spreads across the faces of the grand jurors.

"Mr. Cox, do you have any response?" Judge Sirica asks.

"Your honor," begins Cox, "I sought highly relevant material to the investigation, and specific tapes at the request of the grand jury. I now request that you issue an Order to Show Cause for compliance."

Judge Sirica nods. This is exactly what he has anticipated. An Order to Show Cause requires a party to immediately comply with the court order—the subpoena in this case—or to appear in court and explain fully the reasons for not complying. Noncompliance with a court order is a cause to charge someone with contempt of court, and that can result in a prison sentence or fine.

"Is the foreman here? Please step forward, Mr. Pregelj." Judge Sirica motions to him.

Over the course of the past year since the Watergate grand jury was first convened, the judge has gotten to know and respect Vladimir Nicholas Pregelj. He is a refugee from Yugoslavia who works for the National Archives, and has served as the grand jury foreman throughout the Watergate proceedings.

"Do you, Mr. Pregelj, confirm the statement of the special prosecutor?"

"Yes, I do," replies Pregelj.

"Do you, Mr. Pregelj, as foreman of the grand jury convened on this matter, support a request by Special Prosecutor Cox that I sign an Order to Show Cause why there should not be full and prompt compliance with the subpoena of the court to be delivered to President Richard M. Nixon?"

"Yes, I support it, Your Honor."

"Now," Judge Sirica says, "I would like to hear from each and every member of the grand jury. Yes or no, do you support the Order to Show Cause requested by Mr. Cox?"

The judge knows that all of this is unusual. He wants to underscore that it's not just the judge or the special prosecutor, but the people—ordinary citizens doing their civic duty—who seek this material.

The clerk polls the other twenty-two grand jurors. All agree.

"So ordered," the judge says.

The Order to Show Cause is delivered to the White House by members of the special prosecutor's team. Judge Sirica realizes, as he straightens his desk in the afternoon, that the rest of the summer is going to be very busy.

Surely the president's lawyers will raise a claim of executive privilege, and it's not a topic about which the judge knows a great deal. In fact, there are few lawyers across the country who know much about it. Matters of robbery, murder, arson, and mayhem are much more likely to come into the judge's courtroom than issues of executive privilege. It is a topic of singular constitutional significance.

The judge searches across the library of books and cases for something, anything, that might give the clues he needs.

"Best cancel your summer plans," he says to Todd. "We're into serious constitutional territory here. And this one is definitely going to go up. I want to get it right."

Todd knows that by "go up" he means "up to the court of appeals." Or even the United States Supreme Court. Todd nods. He understands that while his boss is perfectly willing to make on-the-spot rulings in court like a referee in a ring, this decision is certain to touch upon the very heart of American democracy.

It's no surprise when the president adamantly refuses to deliver the materials sought under the Order to Show Cause. Instead, he hires Charles Alan Wright, a professor from the University of Texas, to represent him on the constitutional matter of executive privilege and the powers of the presidency. Law students and judges alike know about Wright—he is one of the authors of the fifty-four-volume treatise on federal procedure. He will be sparring against Special Prosecutor Cox. They are two of the most knowledgeable and erudite attorneys in the country, and both file briefs on the matter within days.

Wright's thirty-four-page brief on behalf of the president arrives on August 7. He argues that the president has an executive privilege to keep his communications private, and that having to turn over private conversations with his aides will harm the presidency and interfere with the independence of the executive branch. "If the special prosecutor should be successful in the attempt to compel disclosure of recordings of presidential conversations, the damage to the institution of the presidency will be severe and irreparable," the brief states. Additionally, Wright points out, there is the practical matter: How would a subpoena against the president be enforced?

Reading the brief in chambers, Judge Sirica pokes his index finger at that line. Of course, it's true. The courts can make decisions, but they don't have a police force to enforce them; the courts are entirely dependent upon the Executive Office for law enforcement. But the implicit threat—that the president will not obey the order of a court? Hard to imagine.

Special Prosecutor Cox delivers his brief the following week, this one sixty-eight pages in length. He makes the case that everyone is subject to the rule of law, even the president, and that the president should not be allowed to decide, on his own, the scope of executive privilege. Failure to have access to the tapes would withhold material evidence from the grand jury and frustrate the prosecution of suspected criminal misconduct. "Confidence in our institutions is at stake," Cox asserts.

On August 26, the two constitutional law scholars meet in court to present their cases personally before Judge Sirica. All 350 seats in the Ceremonial Courtroom are filled.

Charles Alan Wright, stretching to his full height of six-foot-three, expounds on the independence of the Executive Office. He has a new argument, too: national security.

"The president has told me that in one of the tapes, there is national security material so sensitive that he would not feel free even to mention to me what the nature of the material is," Wright declares. Production of the tapes would, he says, "cripple the powers of the presidency."

"Mr. Wright," Judge Sirica says, "in light of the White House claim that the president is the sole judge of his own privilege, isn't such absolute power contrary to the spirit of checks and balances that we find in the Constitution?"

"The framers of the Constitution provided a remedy for abuses of presidential power," Wright responds, "but this is in the impeachment procedure in Congress."

Cox, given his turn at the podium, is fierce. "There is strong reason to believe that the integrity of the Executive Office has been corrupted," he says. "No one, not even the president, has the absolute power to arbitrarily decide on his own say-so what will be disclosed to the courts, especially in a case involving conversations that were apparently poisoned by criminality." The tapes are critical to resolving differing accounts of discussions with the president, he explains.

After two-and-a-half hours, Judge Sirica gavels the session to a close.

"Thank you both, gentlemen, for a masterful exposition of the issues at stake." He announces that he will issue an opinion in a week.

That afternoon, President Nixon holds a press conference

at the "Western White House"—his California home in San Clemente.

"Watergate is an episode I deeply deplore, but it's water under the bridge now. We must move on from Watergate to the business of the people," he says. He rebuts John Dean's testimony again, and states, unequivocally, that he has no intention of resigning.

Judge Sirica and Todd immediately dive into full-out research. Part-time clerk Richard Azzaro is put to work, too.

"I want you to each take one side and write up an opinion as if it were from that perspective," Judge Sirica tells them. "Then we will be able to feel where the strengths and weaknesses lie."

The next day, Todd and the judge take a mid-afternoon break and go for a walk around the block, passing by the fifteen-foot-high statue of the historic legal scholar Blackstone outside the E. Barrett Prettyman courthouse.

"Something bothers me," Judge Sirica says. "If the president did nothing wrong, why not turn over the tapes and put the matter to rest?"

"I agree. But what if—and according to Charles Wright, it's true—confidential or national security matters are on the tapes?"

Todd's sincerity is something that the judge likes—it's one of the reasons he picked him for the law clerk position.

"But we need to think about the integrity of the courts. People need to believe that the courts aren't in on some kind of whitewash," says Judge Sirica.

"We don't have much precedent to go on other than Justice Marshall and the Aaron Burr case," Todd offers.

"Yes, yes," Judge Sirica responds. "The only other time in history that a judge issued a subpoena to a president—166 years ago. Cox referred to it when he sought the subpoena, but now I've done some digging and I know it like the shape of my fist. The trial of Aaron Burr—charged with treason for allegedly attempting to organize a militia to seize western territories. Judge John Marshall signs a subpoena for a letter from President Jefferson as evidence. Jefferson denies that he is obligated to follow the subpoena, but ultimately produces the letter anyhow with private information removed. Solved by compromise."

"But President Nixon is refusing to budge. He's claiming an absolute privilege to decide what he should be able to make public, if I read Wright's brief correctly," Todd says.

"I'm thinking of something else now, and it's the judicial branch. All kinds of my cases have claims of privilege. A wife and a husband, a priest and a confessant, a lawyer and a client. Nothing is absolute. The grand jury has a right to every man's evidence."

"I see what you mean," Todd says.

"There are plenty of balancing tests for introducing evidence for other privileged communications. That's what we need. We need to create a new balancing test for the introduction of evidence from the president." The judge waves his hand in the air and turns on his heel to go back to the courthouse, letting Todd catch up. "Plan to come in over the weekend. I'll be here," the judge says over his shoulder.

On Wednesday, August 29, the weather is hot and thick with smog as Judge Sirica drives to the courthouse. Along the way, he steadies his mind for the task ahead. They've worked all weekend, and stayed late on Monday and Tuesday. He's arisen extra early to read over the opinion and make more changes. Normally, he doesn't agonize over what the court of appeals will do—he does his job, they do theirs. Sometimes, they agree with him;

sometimes they find error. He generally lets it roll off his back. This time, he wants to get every detail right.

When Judge Sirica enters the courtroom in his robe, the room is already packed.

The bailiff calls the case: "In re Grand Jury *Subpoena Duces Tecum* Issued to Richard M. Nixon, or any Subordinate Officer, Official, or Employee with Custody or Control of Certain Documents or Objects."

Judge Sirica positions himself and puts on his glasses. "The Court," he reads—referring to himself, the decision maker—"is extremely reluctant to finally stand against a declaration of the President of the United States on any but the strongest possible evidence."

He continues to read through twenty-three pages. "The grand jury has a right to every man's evidence and . . . for purposes of gathering evidence, process may issue to anyone . . . . The court cannot say that the Executive's persistence in withholding the tape recordings would 'tarnish its reputation,' but must admit that it would tarnish the Court's reputation to fail to do what it could in pursuit of justice . . . . In all candor, the Court fails to perceive any reason for suspending the power of the courts to get evidence and rule on questions of privilege in criminal matters simply because it is the President of the United States who holds the evidence.

"The Court is simply unable to decide the question of privilege without inspecting the tapes," the judge reads from his pages. "The Court has attempted to walk the middle ground between a failure to decide the question of privilege at one extreme and a wholesale delivery of tapes to the grand jury at the other. The one would be a breach of duty; the other an inexcusable course of conduct."

To balance competing needs, the judge orders the tapes released, but states that they will be delivered to him first, and he will listen to them privately—*in camera* is the Latin term. The president's team will highlight in advance claims of national security or confidentiality. The judge will then determine if any confidential or national security interests will be compromised and those portions will be eliminated before the material is released to the special prosecutor or to the grand jury.

"Executive fiat," the judge says, "is not the mode of resolution."

How the case will be received becomes evident the next day when the judge picks up his morning paper. The *Washington Post*, at the top of the page, running from one margin to the next, declares "JUDGE RULES AGAINST PRESIDENT: Sirica Wants to Listen to Nine Tapes." A headshot picture of the judge, in white shirt and striped tie, is in the lead position on the upper right. The judge imagines, briefly, the newsboys he worked with so many years ago on the streets of Washington, D.C., barking out the headlines . . . and now here he is in the prime bellowing-out position. Never, as a newsboy, could he have imagined himself on the front page.

The full text of the opinion is published on three interior pages. There's also a profile of him, emphasizing his days as a boxing instructor while attending law school.

The president's response is in the third paragraph of the front-page story: "The White House said flatly that Mr. Nixon 'will not comply with this order.'" The president states that an *in camera* review of the tapes is not consistent with his view of the separation of powers.

Chapter Fifteen

A HIGHER POWER

When the president files a challenge to the decision on the tapes in the court of appeals, Judge Sirica is unable to sleep at all. He's anxious about the ruling of the appellate court. This feels momentous; this feels like the most important fight of his life. The briefs and arguments are left to the litigants—the lawyers for the president, and the special prosecutor.

The oral hearing is on September 11, and Judge Sirica grabs the first newspaper accounts to read about it. Seven federal appellate judges hear the case in the same Ceremonial Courtroom on the sixth floor where the burglary trial was held. Charles Wright makes a strong argument for the president, suggesting the problem is not the president's willingness to provide information—and implying he might do so voluntarily—but the grave need to safeguard the presidency itself. An order from the court requiring delivery of the tapes would do "great damage to the presidency," he says—there would be no limit on what could be demanded from a president, a violation of the separation of powers.

Two days later, the court of appeals responds in an unusual way. It issues a memorandum urging the president and the special prosecutor to come up with an out-of-court agreement. The idea, it seems, is to follow the example in the case of President Jefferson and Aaron Burr and avoid a constitutional tussle. They try. Then on September 20 comes the next report to the court of appeals: no agreement is possible. The matter is dropped back into the lap of the appellate court.

Judge Sirica's apprehension, like that of the general public, increases with other looming scandals at the White House. Questions are raised about hundreds of thousands of dollars of government funds spent on properties owned by President Nixon in California and Florida. Newspaper stories say that the president amassed large sums of money from unknown sources while serving in the White House, but he paid virtually no taxes. There is a second grand jury empanelled in August to look at associated issues that have emerged—illegal campaign contributions, White House pressure on the government's settlement of an International Telephone and Telegraph antitrust case, and improper influence in setting milk-price supports. Then there is the matter of Vice President Spiro Agnew. Amid charges of corruption, payoffs, and bribes, he resigns on October 10 and is sentenced in a Baltimore federal court on a felony charge of income tax evasion. The president soon signals his intention to nominate Representative Gerald Ford of Michigan to replace Agnew as vice president.

On October 12, Judge Sirica goes looking for Todd in the courthouse library on the third floor and finds him sitting at a wooden table. Holding a pile of fax pages high in his left hand, the judge punches Todd's arm lightly.

"The president's executive privilege is not all-encompassing," the judge says. He can't help but let himself smile a bit.

"Upheld?" Todd presses his hand against his heart. He hasn't been sleeping well, either.

"The Appeals Court agrees with our reasoning," the judge says. He emphasizes the word "our"—Todd's careful research and drafting helped polish the ruling. "The president is ordered to turn over the tapes for review. Five judges out of seven. Including Chief Judge Bazelon. And J. Skelly Wright. The two most respected! Listen to this: 'The president does not embody the nation's sovereignty. He is not above the law's commands.' No absolute privilege. The president has an executive privilege, but it's the role of the courts to set limits on the executive privilege. 'The want of physical power' to enforce court judgments is no argument against rendering them. 'Even the chief executive is subject to the mandate of law.'"

Todd scans through the forty-seven-page decision for himself. "This has never happened before—the president ordered to turn over evidence to the court."

"For every time the court of appeals has overturned my rulings—and there have been plenty—it feels remarkably good to have them on my side this time."

"Do you think the president's lawyers will appeal to the Supreme Court?" Todd asks the obvious.

"Of course, of course. But at least we won this one," Judge Sirica says. "And on the Christopher Columbus anniversary."

The Lido Civic Club marks the anniversary of Columbus's landing every year with a special event, but the judge is skipping it this year. Like a lot of his personal life, day-to-day engagements are getting thrown by the wayside. It's almost as if he's sequestered himself—he doesn't want to be questioned by the hordes of curious people, whether friends, neighbors, lawyers, or reporters. "I'm not that kind. This is a case-in-process," he tells the press people who catch him in the hallway of the courthouse.

He does manage to get some clips of the articles together for Jack Dempsey and addresses an envelope to the popular restaurant that the former boxer now owns in Times Square. The judge writes a note in fountain pen across the top of the page:

> *Thank you for your supportive words for me over the years. I can't tell you how much this decision means to me. Upheld!*

Chapter Sixteen

SHIFTING WATERS

With an all-but-certain appeal to the Supreme Court on the tapes decision—the court of appeals gives the president five business days to file the initial notice, and then it will take plenty of time for the briefs to be prepared by the parties and the high court to review the matter—Judge Sirica decides to take a family day, finally.

After the morning court session on Friday, October 19, he heads to Connecticut with his oldest daughter, Patricia, to look at a college that interests her; she's graduating at the end of the next school year. A long weekend away from legal turmoil is just what he needs.

He's not even gone one night when the president announces that he doesn't intend to appeal. The judge is familiar with Friday night news releases—that's when all politicians like to put out statements on controversial matters, figuring that most everyone is away. The president also says that he does not plan to comply with the decision by the court of appeals requiring him to turn over the tapes to Judge Sirica for review.

Instead, the president says, he will deliver edited summaries of the tapes, along with the actual tapes, to Senator John C. Stennis of Mississippi. Senator Stennis, a longtime supporter of the president, will review the material and verify that the summaries are accurate, and then the summaries will be sent to the special prosecutor and the Senate Watergate Committee. The president calls this the "Stennis Compromise."

The president goes one step further: he orders Special Prosecutor Cox to take no further court action "to compel production of recordings, notes, or memoranda regarding private presidential conversations."

The Stennis Compromise is not at all consistent with the decision from the court of appeals. Special Prosecutor Cox rejects it. He tells the president on Friday that he can't accept something that voluntarily limits the investigative power of the grand jury. Nor is he going to allow a third party of the president's choosing to substantiate the tapes. Without the actual tapes and verifiable word-for-word transcripts to submit to the court—the "highest and best evidence"—none of the information will be admissible in a trial.

On Saturday, Cox holds a televised news conference from the National Press Building, explaining why he can't accept the president's declaration. "I think it is my duty as the special prosecutor, as an officer of the court, and as a representative of the grand jury to bring to the court's attention what seems to be noncompliance with the court's order," he states. Despite the president's order that he do nothing further, Cox explains that he will return to Judge Sirica's courtroom to seek a decision on whether the president has violated the ruling of the court of appeals.

Sitting in Connecticut, the judge can only watch from afar. He has no library and no law books, and he cannot be reached readily. He scribbles notes on a pad from the hotel.

Saturday afternoon turns into a dizzying spectacle. The TV news carries bulletins. The president's new chief of staff, Alexander Haig, orders Attorney General Elliot Richardson to fire Special Prosecutor Archibald Cox because of his defiance of the president's order to accept the Stennis Compromise and drop any further court proceedings on the tapes. Rather than fire the special prosecutor, Richardson resigns.

Haig then orders the Deputy Attorney General William Ruckelshaus to fire Special Prosecutor Cox. Ruckelshaus, too, refuses and resigns.

Next in line at the Justice Department is Robert Bork, the solicitor general. The president appoints him the acting attorney general, and at 8 p.m. on Saturday, Bork fires Special Prosecutor Cox.

Reporters immediately dub it the "Saturday Night Massacre."

Is this all to avoid the judge's order to deliver the tapes? Judge Sirica's mind is churning. The Stennis Compromise is absurd—Cox was entirely right to reject it. As a judge in the courtroom, he would never accept evidence like a summary of a tape reviewed by a personally selected third party. He mentally reels back to the FCC hearings and the efforts to manipulate the evidence.

Then, at 8:24 p.m., the president's spokesperson, Ronald Ziegler, appears at a special night briefing of the press and announces that not only has the special prosecutor been dismissed, but the entire office of the special prosecutor is being disbanded. "The functions of the special prosecutor are returned to the Department of Justice," Ziegler says.

The TV shows scenes from the K Street NW office of the special prosecutor, where the FBI is taking control of files like it's a banana republic, removing the staff and locking them out.

"Unbelievable," Judge Sirica says out loud in his hotel room to no one in particular.

But there is no way he is going to allow the courts to be treated in the same manner. Not on his life. With Patricia bubbling about her potential college plans, Judge Sirica begins to chart out possible judicial responses in his mind.

On Sunday morning, the judge is able to get the *New York Times* from the hotel newsstand and sees that the response across the country echoes his own. There, in eight columns across the entire front page, in all capital letters, is a three-line headline usually reserved for declarations of war: "NIXON DISCHARGES COX FOR DEFIANCE; ABOLISHES WATERGATE TASK FORCE; RICHARDSON AND RUCKELSHAUS OUT."

Oval Office switchboards are flooded with calls. Crowds of protestors gather in front of the White House. Telegrams and letters are pouring into the Capitol. Members of the House of Representatives are advocating impeachment, but it's only some members—not enough to make it stick. The newspaper describes the events as "the most traumatic government upheaval of the Watergate crisis."

Judge Sirica fixes his sights on the next court hearing: the upcoming Tuesday, October 23. No person is above the law. If he has to be the backstop for the courts, then by all means, he will be it. It's like preparing for a fight. He's in shape; he feels confident about what he will do. His mind is focused.

As soon as he returns to the courthouse on Monday, Judge Sirica begins preparing an order that he will release in court the next day. It will be firm. It will be decisive. His plan is to hold the president in contempt of court. In some cases, contempt of court results in arrest—that's what the judge did in the case of the Ku Klux Klan leader who refused to testify in Congress. That won't work when the party at hand is the President of the United States. But he has another idea: He will fine the president a hefty amount—$25,000 to $50,000 a day—for each day that he fails to comply with the order to turn over the tapes. Money talks, and Richard Nixon understands that. In this case, Judge Sirica will offer one more warning, and then apply the fine.

A raft of letters and telegrams also arrives in his chambers, reflective of the national uproar. People exhort him to stick to his guns, uphold the order, take action. It's all well and good, but this is quite possibly the deepest conflict in the history of the nation between the judicial and executive branches of government—it's not to be taken lightly.

As he mounts the bench on Tuesday, the judge prepares for the president's lawyer, Charles Wright, to expound on his justification for the Stennis Compromise. But when Wright stands, that's not what he says.

"I am authorized to say that the President of the United States will comply with the court's order in all respects," Wright says.

The judge looks up from his prepared notes to make sure that he has heard Wright correctly. After a beat, he replies, "Mr. Wright, the court is very happy the president has reached this decision." Without even being aware of it, he smiles.

Wright promises that the tapes will be indexed and delivered to Judge Sirica—"as expeditiously as possible."

Back in his chambers, the judge puts his contempt order away, unsigned and undelivered, before lying down on a couch for a few minutes. These past few days have drained him to the point of exhaustion. But at least, like a bad nightmare, the crisis has passed.

The waters become muddier the next week when White House lawyer J. Fred Buzhardt attends a meeting in the judge's chambers to plan transfer of the tapes.

Buzhardt, with the title of assistant White House counsel, is a West Point graduate who had worked on Capitol Hill for Senator Strom Thurmond of his home state of South Carolina and as a lawyer at the Department of Defense. Unassuming and with military politeness, he is handling the day-to-day legal matters related to Watergate.

As lawyers from all sides parse out the mundane details of how the tapes will be physically delivered to Judge Sirica, Buzhardt clears his throat. "Of the nine tapes," he says, "I must report—"

"Speak up, Mr. Buzhardt." Judge Sirica swings his office chair in Buzhardt's direction.

"I must report, that two . . . it seems that two . . . are non-existent."

"Nonexistent? What the devil does that mean?" the judge demands.

"Missing. Not to be found."

"What! Where are they?"

"It seems they were never made, Your Honor."

"How can that be? After all these months of discussions about them? Since July? Subpoena? Order to Show Cause? Courtroom hearings? Written opinion? Appeal to the court of appeals? Arguments of Charles Alan Wright? Firing of the special prosecutor? And never mentioned once before?"

"That's why I'm telling you now, sir."

"But the White House assured the court previously that they were in a safe place."

"Yes, Your Honor, that's true. But now I've learned otherwise with respect to these two."

"Which two tapes are 'nonexistent'?"

"Well, sir, that would be the telephone conversation on June 20, 1972, between the president and Mr. Mitchell."

"That's three days after the break-in."

"Yes. And the second tape that's missing is for the evening of April 15, 1973, of a meeting between the president and John Dean in the Executive Office Building next to the White House."

"Do you have an explanation for this?"

"It's possible that the recording mechanisms were not working properly. Or, on the phone, that the president was speaking on a different line without recording devices attached." Buzhardt adjusts his glasses and looks down at the floor.

"Ridiculous. Be in my courtroom tomorrow morning, first thing. We will put this on the record. At once. And I want a full inquiry into the whereabouts of these tapes. Be prepared to call relevant witnesses—guardians of the tapes, anyone who has handled them or has listened to them, logs. A to Z. Do you hear me?"

"Yes, sir."

The courtroom hearings on the missing tapes bring more attention to the issue. It turns out that a Dictabelt of the April 15 meeting, supposedly reviewed by the president and about which he disclosed information to the Senate Watergate Committee, is also missing.

With this news lapping on the heels of the Saturday Night Massacre, a new drumbeat for impeachment rises. The president shifts course again. Although he had fired Cox and announced the closure of the office of the special prosecutor, suddenly he names a new special prosecutor: Leon Jaworski. Jaworski, a successful corporate lawyer from Texas, is a George Washington University law graduate and a one-time prosecutor of Nazi war crimes. He's spent time in Washington serving on several federal commissions as an appointee of President Lyndon Johnson and is the former president of the American Bar Association.

The newspapers are full of polls on President Nixon's popularity—it's sinking. Although Nixon seems to prefer being cloistered in the White House, he is now making appearances across the country, part of what he is calling "Operation Candor," an effort to be straight with the American people.

In one speech in Florida, the president tells the audience, "In all of my years of public life, I have never profited—never profited—from public service. I earned every cent. And in all of my years of public life, I have never obstructed justice . . . . People have got to know whether or not their president is a crook. Well, I'm not a crook." The last phrase quickly enters the lexicon of opinion-page cartoonists and late-night comedians.

On November 21, the day before Thanksgiving, Fred Buzhardt requests an emergency meeting with the judge and the new special prosecutor, Jaworski.

"Judge, we have a problem," Buzhardt says. "There is one tape, Your Honor, that I've learned has an eighteen-and-a-half-minute obliteration of the intelligence."

An erasure. This eighteen-and-a-half-minute gap is on a tape made on June 20, 1972—three days after the Watergate break-in. The president's longtime personal secretary, Rose Mary Woods, says that she made the erasure accidentally. The discussion, according to notes by then-chief of staff Bob Haldeman, addresses the Watergate break-in. By existing timelines, this is the first time that Nixon discussed the incident with his staff. Curiously, all of the discussion of Watergate is missing.

"Let's discuss this in court. Four p.m.," Judge Sirica announces at once.

"Your Honor, sir, disclosure could be devastating. We prefer to withhold the news. We need a little time to research this and write it up." Buzhardt sinks back in his chair.

"You have an hour and a half," says the judge.

"But with the holiday tomorrow—"

"We're not going to have any more of this, Mr. Buzhardt. Four p.m. You can use the courthouse library upstairs." The judge stands and gestures with his open palm to the door.

Todd, sitting in, understands exactly what the judge is doing: getting it on the record as soon as possible. Just like the McCord letter. Just like Nixon's letter. Just like the other missing tapes. He knows what the judge will do in court: demand the full reels of the subpoenaed tapes to be deposited with the court at once to prevent any further disappearances or erasures.

At the hearing that afternoon, the White House concedes that from here on in, Judge Sirica will safeguard the subpoenaed tapes. On the Monday after the hearing, a construction crew comes to the judge's chambers and installs a super-tight safe supplied by the National Security Agency. The tapes are delivered under strict security and locked away. United States Marshals are posted outside the door on a twenty-four-hour basis. Closed-circuit cameras are added to monitor the area.

The judge orders experts to examine the tape with the

eighteen-and-a-half-minute gap, and commences with hearings on it immediately. If the president's lawyers thought making the announcement about the eighteen-and-a-half-minute gap on a "dead" news day would bury the story, they were wrong.

Rose Mary Woods, a lifelong Nixon ally, is suddenly catapulted into the limelight. Testifying in court, Woods says that she erased a critical portion of the tape when a phone five feet away rang while she was transcribing. Reaching to answer the phone, she accidentally left her foot on an operating pedal of the tape recorder while simultaneously, and erroneously, pushing a "record" button. Asked to demonstrate this in court, it proves to be nearly impossible to accomplish physically.

Overnight, the White House tries to fix this perception by recreating the moment in Woods' office for in-house photographers. But Woods is stretched so far forward that she looks like a baseball player sliding toward home. TV host Johnny Carson later jokes that a belly dancer is invited to a state dinner with the president: "Mr. Nixon was really impressed. He hadn't seen contortions like that since Rose Mary Woods."

In court, Judge Sirica sees less humor. He's more worried about potential obstruction of justice and tampering with evidence. Woods' phone conversation had lasted only five and a half minutes, she says. "I must emphasize that I was not on the phone for eighteen and a half minutes," she states. Even this rendition of events, if accepted, leaves thirteen minutes unaddressed.

White House Chief of Staff Alexander Haig says that perhaps Woods didn't know how long she had talked on the phone. He says that he knows women who often think they've only chatted for a few minutes but have talked longer. Barring that, he tries another theory to explain the unexplained thirteen minutes.

"Perhaps," he says, "some sinister force had come in and . . . taken care of the information on that tape."

Judge Sirica scowls. "Has anyone ever suggested who that sinister force might be?" he asks from the bench.

Haig doesn't have an answer.

Buzhardt, testifying under oath, says the eighteen-and-a-half-minute gap had not been reported previously because the White House mistakenly believed that it wasn't covered under the subpoena until Buzhardt did a careful rereading of it.

Judge Sirica turns his chair fully to address Buzhardt in the witness box. "You mean to say that it takes a careful reading to conclude that the subpoena called for the conversation of Mr. Haldeman and Mr. Ehrlichman between 10:30 a.m. and 12:45 p.m.?"

"In my opinion, Your Honor, it takes a very careful reading," Buzhardt replies, speaking softly into the microphone in front of him.

The White House soon announces that another lawyer, James St. Clair of Boston, is replacing him.

Six experts who examine the tape with the gap return with the information that the erasures have been done and redone at least five times, and that hand manipulation of the tape equipment was required. The information on it can't be recovered.

"This is crazy," Judge Sirica says to Todd in chambers. "Every witness has a different story about the erasure, and none of the stories make sense. We know from the experts that it was deliberate, but beyond that . . . who, what, how? Fact is, we may never know." He swiftly ties the brown strings to close up a binder of documents in front of him.

"Is there anything more to do about it?"

"I think we've turned over all the stones we can. I'll suggest that the special prosecutor and the grand jury take up this matter since there is a distinct possibility of unlawful conduct on the part of someone—or several someones. Right now, we need to focus on the evidence that we do have. Let's finalize the arrangements for listening to the tapes."

Over the next week, Judge Sirica reviews the claims of privilege and confidentiality filed by the White House. Four tapes have no claim of privilege whatsoever, so they are delivered posthaste to the special prosecutor.

To review the other tapes, the judge's jury room is fitted up with listening devices. The White House sends over a machine. The CIA delivers another machine that can enhance the quality of the tapes. At the judge's request, there are two sets of headphones so that the judge and Todd can plug in and no one outside can overhear anything. The judge asks the FBI to do one final check of the room to make sure that no one has planted electronic bugs. At last, they are ready to listen.

John and Todd come in on the second Saturday in December. The courthouse is barren, and both of them have dressed casually to settle in. Their footsteps echo as they walk down the polished hall to the judge's chambers and through the courtroom to the jury room. Todd fixes a tape reel from March 13, 1973, onto the machine and they put on the headsets. As their ears adjust to the sound, the voices of the speakers in the Oval Office come to life. They are transported at once to the White House, to the seat of power, the center of all the discussions they've been having for the past year and a half. They sit, each with their notes of the claims of privilege from the White House, ready for the very serious task of ascertaining which segments should be withheld from evidence.

After they listen for a moment, Judge Sirica shakes his head.

This isn't what he expected. His eyes drop over to Todd, and he almost wants to apologize.

President Nixon's voice is unmistakable. But the words are crass and coarse, the kind of gutter language that the judge might have heard at his father's pool hall. Nixon swears constantly. He calls people names—ugly and disdainful depictions of people— quite unlike the public Nixon for whom the judge had campaigned at one point, and cast his vote for at other times. He spits out orders that seem laced with mendacity.

But it's the actual content that's the most frightening. At every turn, the president gives ideas about what actions his staff should take, and none of them align with following the law, going to proper authorities, making illegal conduct public. Instead, he is intent on covering up the Watergate incident. Never once does he express concern about the criminal activities, or regret for them. There is no effort to identify wrongdoers, clear the house of bad actors, or set his subordinates straight from a wayward path. Instead, he joins them in scheming about ways to evade the law.

Judge Sirica dashes a note onto a pad in front of him:

Oath of Office: The president swears to uphold the Constitution and the laws of the United States!!!

On one tape from March 22, 1973, Nixon meets with Haldeman, Ehrlichman, Mitchell, and Dean. The president says, "I don't give a s*** what happens. I want you all to stonewall it, let them plead the Fifth Amendment, cover up, or anything else."

After they finish listening to two tapes, the judge removes his headphones. "Perhaps we should give it a break."

Todd nods, slowly packs up the equipment, and locks away the tapes. "I didn't expect . . . ." He stops.

"Neither did I," says Judge Sirica.

They walk along slowly to the courthouse parking lot, heads down, no further words passing between them. The seasonal Christmas parties are beginning, but they aren't really in the spirit.

On Monday, they continue. Todd keys up the two-hour tape of the March 21 meeting between John Dean and the president—the discussion about which Dean gave extensive testimony to the Senate Watergate Committee. Dean says that he told the president there was "a cancer" on the presidency and described each event in the post-Watergate cover-up. The president, Dean says, showed knowledge of the activities, and pitched in new ideas about how to overcome obstacles. The president disputes Dean's account thoroughly. In its own way, this is the conversation of Dean versus Nixon that led to the urgent demand for the tapes in the first place.

On the tape, Dean talks about "a cancer" on the presidency, as he had described, and goes through a litany of cover-up and payoff activities. The president doesn't balk when Dean says that one million dollars will be needed in payoff cash; in fact, he says it's not a problem. To hear it in his own words, Judge Sirica has no doubt that the president isn't joking, as he later tried to claim.

Dean explains that Howard Hunt is making threats that amount to blackmail if he doesn't get $120,000, and very soon.

The president replies, "Don't you think you have to handle Hunt's financial situation? . . . Damn soon. Either that or let it all blow right now . . . That's why you, for your immediate thing, you've got no choice with Hunt but the hundred and twenty or whatever it is. Right?"

"Right," replies Dean on the tape.

"Would you agree," the president continues, "that that's a buy-time thing you better damned well get that done, but fast?"

After Judge Sirica and Todd listen, the judge, still wearing his headphones, slides a piece of paper over to Todd. "Would it not be advisable to hear the complete tape again?" it says.

Todd puts the reel on for a second listen.

When they complete the run, the judge removes his headphones. His face is expressionless, his voice is muted. "There's Dean's corroboration."

Todd stares at the tape recorder. He's been a Nixon fan and supporter, too. "I wonder what the new special prosecutor will think. Mr. Jaworski."

"Yes. It'll be in his hands soon. The highest and best evidence," the judge says.

They both sit, unmoving, for a few minutes, and decide to leave early.

Chapter Seventeen

THE EXPANDING SCOPE

Judge Sirica has the remaining tapes delivered to Special Prosecutor Jaworski on December 19 after removal of segments that he has determined are protected by executive privilege.

But the eighteen-and-a-half-minute gap, preceded by Nixon's refusal to turn over the tapes and the Saturday Night Massacre, has ripped open a fissure in public opinion. Operation Candor is cancelled, and by February 6, the House of Representatives passes resolution H.R. 803, giving the House Judiciary Committee authority to investigate impeachment. Under the guidance of the chair, Representative Peter W. Rodino Jr. of New Jersey, the House, like the Senate and the grand jury, enters the process of collecting and reviewing evidence.

Late in February, Jaworski informs Judge Sirica that the Watergate grand jury has new indictments. Receiving indictments from the grand jury is part of the job of the chief judge.

On March 1, the second-floor courtroom is packed with reporters when the grand jurors are led in by the U.S. Marshal.

Since there are more than twenty of them, the grand jurors don't fit in the regular jury box and are seated in the spectator section. In the hallway outside the courtroom, scores of hopeful observers line up to get a view—most never make it inside.

Once the names are called, longtime deputy court clerk James Capitanio asks the foreman to rise. Vladimir Pregelj, dressed in a tan suit with a dark brown tie, steps forward.

"Your Honor, the grand jury has one indictment and one report that is sealed."

The indictment is handed to Capitanio. Pregelj gives Todd a large manila envelope, sealed, while also pulling up a briefcase from the floor and passing it along.

The indictment specifies twenty-four charges of obstruction of justice, conspiracy, and perjury. It names seven individuals, all close to or working for President Nixon: Bob Haldeman and John Ehrlichman, previously the president's two closest aides; John Mitchell, the former attorney general and the highest-ranking cabinet official ever to be indicted; Charles Colson, once White House special counsel; Robert Mardian, a deputy to Mitchell; Kenneth Parkinson, a lawyer at the Republican Committee; and Gordon Strachan, an assistant to Haldeman. They're quickly dubbed the "Watergate cover-up defendants."

The number of people involved is mounting. In addition to the seven men tried in the burglary case, four other members of the Nixon campaign or administration have already pleaded guilty—John Dean and Jeb Magruder among them.

But the manila envelope from the grand jury is atypical for proceedings like this, and something of a mystery. Todd hands it and the briefcase to Judge Sirica.

"For the official record, I now have this sealed grand jury report, which I will read myself. I will not read it out loud," the judge says. He uses a letter opener to break the seal on the envelope and puts on his glasses to flip through the two pages inside.

Todd steals a quick glance at the judge. If there's one thing that he knows about his boss, it's that he wants to put everything on the record. But he's not doing it now with the letter in front of him. Something particularly unusual must be underfoot.

One of the prosecutors stands. "Your Honor, there is additional material which is referenced in the sealed document in this." He hoists a second bulging briefcase, this one brown. "This is locked and the key is sealed in an envelope within the envelope Your Honor has opened."

"Very well," the judge says as he secures the papers back in the envelope. "The court will, at the conclusion of these proceedings, place these materials in a safe place until further order of this court on their disposition."

It takes the *Washington Post* reporters less than a day to surmise—"according to informed sources"—that the document in the envelope names Richard Nixon as being involved in the conspiracy to obstruct justice. The sealed letter, the newspaper says, has fifty paragraphs depicting the evidence against the president.

They are not far off. The letter lists the facts that connect President Nixon to the cover-up but it then goes on to request that the judge deliver the information, along with supporting evidence in the briefcases, to the House Judiciary Committee considering impeachment—that's also very unusual, almost without precedent. Judge Sirica cannot think of a time when a grand jury has asked him to send a report to Congress.

"What we are left with, then, with respect to the president," note the editorial writers at the *Washington Post*, "is an impeachment process underway in the House and a strong presumption that Judge Sirica has in hand some material which bears in some fashion on the role and conduct of the president. A great deal rides on what it is that Judge Sirica finds in the sealed material and what he determines to be the proper use for it."

For the next two weeks, Judge Sirica reviews the materials that the grand jury has compiled, and announces that he will render an opinion on them in court on March 18.

As he passes through his chambers to the courtroom to read the opinion, the judge's birthday is also on his mind—it's a big one and only a day away. He stops by the desk of his longtime secretary, Mrs. Holley.

"We'll have to change all my stationery," he says, pointing to the line that says "Chief Judge."

"Not until tomorrow, Your Honor. And you don't fool me—you'll be seventy years *young* whether that's the mandatory retirement age for the 'Chief' or not."

"Those circles under my eyes in the newspaper didn't make me look young. I looked like a raccoon."

"Well, I'm ready, in any case." She reaches into her bottom drawer to pull out a box of stationery, and points to "Senior Judge" where "Chief Judge" had been. "I read the court news today, too, so I suspect I'll be using it a lot."

"Ah. So ya know that I assigned the Watergate cover-up case—Mitchell, Haldeman, Ehrlichman, and all that lot— before I let go of the 'Chief' designation."

"Yes. And according to the court news, I believe that you assigned the case of *United States v. Mitchell et. al* to 'Senior Judge' Sirica."

"I hope he'll do a passable job of it." The judge straightens the knot of the tie under his robe. "After a year and nine months, who knows Watergate better? Circles under my eyes or not, the wheels inside are still working." He waves his opinion at her and heads to the bench with the pages she's typed.

In open court, he confirms that the grand jury report in the sealed envelope and two briefcases that accompany it indeed focus on the President of the United States, as the newspapers had ventured. As such, he says, the information is important to the work of the House Judiciary Committee, and the items will be sent to the committee as the grand jury has requested.

"It should not be forgotten that we deal in a most critical moment to the nation, an impeachment investigation involving the President of the United States," he says. "It would be difficult to conceive of a more compelling need than that of this country for an unswervingly fair inquiry based on all the pertinent information."

Within days, two lawyers from the House Judiciary Committee, accompanied by a squad of police, take the briefcases from the safe of the now "Senior Judge" Sirica and carry them away.

There's not much time to relax. New evidentiary matters continue to arise. It's about tapes again. Both the House Judiciary Committee and Special Prosecutor Jaworski want more tapes of the president's conversations. The White House is not complying. In the second week of April, the House Judiciary Committee changes its request to a subpoena—the first time a Congressional investigation has used the power of subpoena to secure evidence from a president.

Jaworski also wants more tapes for his prosecution of the Watergate cover-up defendants. He has precedent on his side from the decision by the court of appeals. So without much ado, on April 16, he brings Judge Sirica a subpoena for sixty-four tapes of presidential conversations.

"Here we go again," the judge says quietly as he signs the subpoena. Since the court of appeals has already approved the process, he doesn't have a sprinkle of doubt that the procedure is solid.

The White House takes a firm stand against releasing the additional tapes to either Jaworski and the grand jury under Judge Sirica's subpoena or to the House Committee. Three days before the delivery date for Jaworski's subpoena, and one day before the delivery due date on the House subpoena, President Nixon makes his next announcement. Complete with fifty bound green volumes arrayed next to him as props, the president appears on television to declare that instead of delivering the tapes, as subpoenaed, he is releasing 1,254 pages of transcripts typed up by assistants in the White House so that he can "level" with the American people.

"Everything relevant is included," the president says to the cameras. Referring to himself in the third person, he continues: "As far as what the president personally knew and did with regard to Watergate and the cover-up is concerned, these materials, together with those already made available, will tell it all."

Judge Sirica decides to try a test. He compares one of the transcripts produced by the president to a tape already released—among the ones that he and Todd previously reviewed and had sent on to the grand jury. In cross-checking, the judge finds that the president's transcript substitutes every profane word with "EXPLETIVE DELETED." Worse, the transcript conveniently skips over the parts that would be most incriminating of the president.

"They've been sanitized," he says to Todd as they pour over the materials in the jury room.

"At key points," says Todd.

"Of course, it's for show. They don't affect the subpoenas from the special prosecutor."

"So what is the next step, I wonder?"

"I expect we'll be hearing from Mr. Jaworski soon," the judge says.

The release of Nixon's 1,200-plus pages is a publishing sensation—newspapers put out special editions; book companies rush volumes to press. They become instant bestsellers. With even more speed, "expletive deleted" enters the cultural banter: Judge Sirica hears people making "expletive deleted" jokes in the elevator, on his walks, in his occasional listens to Johnny Carson on television.

In early May, it's the White House that is in court. Lawyer James St. Clair, representing the president, wants to get Jaworski's subpoena tossed out. Lawyers for all of the parties—the special prosecutor, the White House, the Watergate cover-up defendants—gather in Judge Sirica's office to review the legal process that will follow.

Jaworski straightens his back against the chair in the center of the room where he is seated. "Since we are in a closed hearing, I want everyone to be aware about one matter decided by the grand jury. We have not previously disclosed this."

Judge Sirica turns sharply in his direction. "What, exactly, is undisclosed, Counselor?"

"The grand jury did not merely issue a 'report' on the president when it indicted Mitchell, Haldeman, Ehrlichman, and the other cover-up defendants. The grand jury named Richard M. Nixon as an *unindicted co-conspirator*. To be clear, the grand jurors actually wanted to indict the president for his involvement in the conspiracy to cover up the Watergate burglary, and they felt that the evidence warranted it. It is my opinion that the Constitution does not permit the president to be indicted while in office. In my research and understanding of the law, the remedy against an errant president is impeachment while he is in office, and impeachment alone. I so advised the grand jury. As a result, the grand jury made the president an unindicted co-conspirator."

Judge Sirica maintains a steely composure. "If I understand you correctly, Mr. Jaworski, the naming of the president as a co-conspirator, although unindicted, means that by criminal law procedure his recorded statements are admissible as evidence in the trial of the other co-conspirators."

"That is our thinking, Your Honor."

"Which makes the tapes highly relevant. Perhaps more relevant." The judge glances over at the bookcase with the code of criminal procedure.

"We would object, of course," says the president's lawyer, James St. Clair.

"Let's get this on the record in the courtroom," Judge Sirica says.

He reaches for a buzzer on his telephone to notify his court clerk and pushes back his chair to find his robe. Watching from the corner of the room, Todd muses at the judge's lifetime habit: Get it on the record.

"Your Honor, with all due respect, we ask that this information remain confidential at this point." Jaworski firmly grips one hand in the other, forming a double fist. "I feel that we needed to make the White House lawyers aware of this matter because they have been indicating that their current objection to the release of additional tapes is that the president is not among the conspirators. But, in fact, he is among the conspirators identified by the grand jury, although he is unindicted. It's still true that public release of this information might prejudice other investigations and hearings."

St. Clair nods his head in agreement. The lawyers for the cover-up defendants nod, too.

"This goes against my better instincts," says Judge Sirica. He remains standing. "I'll hold off—this once. Now get your briefs finalized so I can rule on the subpoena."

St. Clair, representing Nixon, collects his materials and stands to leave. "Be assured that if the president is ordered to deliver more tapes, we will go straight to the court of appeals. Without a moment's delay," he says.

The judge throws up his hand. It's a stalling tactic. The court of appeals has already spoken on this issue.

After St. Clair and the defense lawyers exit, Jaworski lingers for a minute.

"I want you to know, Your Honor, that should the president's lawyers file with the court of appeals, we plan to seek an immediate and direct review by the United States Supreme Court. I know it's not common, but the rules of procedure allow for it when the matter at hand is especially important and deserves a quick resolution. This, Your Honor, fits that definition."

"We'll see where the chips fall, Mr. Jaworski."

On May 20, Judge Sirica issues his decision on the matter. He refuses the president's request to quash the subpoena and orders the president to turn over the additional tapes sought by the special prosecutor.

By May 31, the Supreme Court responds to Jaworski's request for an expedited hearing and, for only the second time since World War II, agrees to hear the case without waiting for the court of appeals. *United States of America v. Richard Nixon, President of the United States* is set for oral arguments in July.

Normally, the Supreme Court justices leave for vacation at the end of June and are gone until September, but this time they are staying in session.

At oral arguments on July 8, Special Prosecutor Jaworski tells the Supreme Court justices why the president should be required to release the tapes listed in Judge Sirica's subpoena, and he describes that the president has been named as an unindicted co-conspirator by the grand jury's unanimous vote. "This nation's constitutional form of government is in serious jeopardy if the president, any president, is to say that the Constitution means what he says it does, and that there is no one, not even the Supreme Court, to tell him otherwise," Jaworski says.

A call to Judge Sirica's chambers on July 24 indicates that the Supreme Court is announcing the decision in *U.S. v. Nixon*—in record time. Todd races over to the Supreme Court building to get a printed copy of the opinion. He speed-reads as much as he can while running back on the grassy Capitol path to Judge Sirica's chambers. He sweeps past Mrs. Holley in the office and bursts into the judge's chambers without knocking.

"I've got it," he says. "Opinion written by Chief Justice Warren E. Burger."

Judge Sirica takes the opinion, puts on his glasses, and reads.

"The very integrity of the judicial system and public confidence in the system depend on full disclosure of all of the facts, within the framework of the rules of evidence.

"The president's broad interest in confidentiality of communications will not be vitiated by disclosure of a limited number of conversations preliminarily shown to have some bearing on the pending criminal case.

"Accordingly, we affirm the order of the District Court that subpoenaed materials be transmitted to that court."

Judge Sirica reads the last line out loud—"We affirm the order of the District Court." His order. Eight judges sign the opinion, none disagree. Thirty-one pages long. Three of the eight justices who concur are Nixon appointees; one Nixon appointee isn't listed because he's removed himself from the case due to conflicts.

The judge takes a little extra time before leaving that day to compose a note to Jack Dempsey.

I've received the news from the Supreme Court.

He writes on stationery that is imprinted with his new "Senior Judge" title.

You'll probably see it in the papers by the time you read this. All of the Supreme Court justices agree with my thinking and they are ordering the president's men to turn over tapes for me to review. A unanimous decision! I can't thank you enough for your confidence in me.

The judge asks Mrs. Holley to post the letter with a photocopy of the opinion's first page.

It's all up to the president and his lawyers now. President Nixon has declared previously that he will comply with a "definitive" decision of the Supreme Court. *This one is about as definitive as it can get,* Judge Sirica thinks.

Two days later, James St. Clair is back in chambers on behalf of the White House.

"It will take time for the president's team to prepare the tapes for delivery," he tells Judge Sirica.

"Did you read the Supreme Court opinion, Counselor?" the judge asks.

"Of course, Your Honor."

"Did you see the part where the Supreme Court said that the tapes should be turned over 'forthwith'?"

"Yes, Your Honor."

"You are a member of the bar, and a member of the Supreme Court bar, are you not?"

"Yes, Your Honor."

"Good. Because I intend to follow the Supreme Court's ruling to the 'T' and to see that is enacted 'forthwith.'"

"I agree, Your Honor. But the tapes need to be prepared and transcribed—"

"Excuse me, Mr. St. Clair. The president himself has already released over 1,200 pages of transcripts. They include, by my clerk's estimation, twenty tapes listed on the subpoena. There is nothing more on them to prepare, then, is there, Mr. St. Clair?"

"Well, no, sir."

"I want those tapes delivered 'forthwith.' Do you understand me, Mr. St. Clair?"

"Yes, Your Honor. I'll see that they you get them. Forthwith."

The House Judiciary Committee has continued its work as well. After months of laborious meetings in the Rayburn Office Building, reviewing in detail 7,200 pages of documents, the committee is ready to vote. By now, the thirty-eight committee members have analyzed 650 points of concern; the evidence in the two bulging briefcases from the grand jury proves to be enormously helpful.

On July 27, 1974, only three days after the Supreme Court decision, people across the country watch on television as the House Judiciary Committee solemnly votes on articles of impeachment.

The first article of impeachment states that the president has "prevented, obstructed, and impeded the administration of justice." It is approved. Six Republicans and all twenty-one Democrats on the committee vote in support.

Two more articles of impeachment are approved in the days that follow: Article Two for abuse of power and disregard of the duty to enforce the Constitution, and Article Three for failing to provide the materials requested by the committee, including the second batch of tapes.

By July 30, the House Judiciary Committee completes its work—three articles of impeachment. The next step will be for the entire House of Representatives to vote on the articles of impeachment. If a majority in the House passes them, the Senate will hold a trial to remove the president from office. A vote of two-thirds of the senators is needed for removal.

Late in the day on July 30, the White House delivers the first twenty tapes to Judge Sirica, as promised. Todd logs them in and places them in the judge's safe. The remaining subpoenaed tapes are sent in the first week of August, although St. Clair is forced to tell Judge Sirica that there are more gaps and more missing tapes.

What St. Clair doesn't report is the turmoil—or perhaps mounting panic—inside the White House about the tapes from June 23, 1972, which are now in the judge's safe. These tapes are of conversations only six days after the Watergate break-in, and three days after the tape with the eighteen-and-a-half-minute gap. Top lawyers in the White House listen to them for the first time and express alarm. The actual conversations are not what has been previously disclosed by the president—they are something much more incriminating.

Confronted with this predicament, President Nixon decides to take a gamble. He releases new transcripts of the conversations from June 23, 1972, along with a two-page statement that explains that portions of the tapes are "at variance with certain of my previous statements." He states that the failure to release the full information about these tapes earlier—even to his lawyers—was "a serious act of omission for which I take full responsibility."

The president says that previously he had relied on his memory, but now he has listened to the tapes. In the past, he'd said that he asked the FBI to coordinate with the CIA on the Watergate incident because he was worried about national security matters. The transcripts paint a different picture. "The June 23 tapes clearly show that at the time I gave those instructions, I also discussed the political aspects of the situation, and that I was aware of the advantages this course of action would have with respect to limiting possible public exposure of involvement by persons connected with the Re-election Committee."

Nixon explains that "the tapes in their entirety are now in the process of being furnished to Judge Sirica. He has begun what may be a rather lengthy process of reviewing the tapes, passing upon specific claims of executive privilege, and forwarding to the special prosecutor those tapes or those portions that are relevant to the Watergate investigation." The president adds that he will voluntarily furnish to the Senate "everything from these tapes that Judge Sirica rules should go to the special prosecutor."

He concludes, "I am firmly convinced that the record, in its entirety, does not justify the extreme step of impeachment and removal of a president. I trust that as the constitutional process goes forward, this perspective will prevail."

What could make these tapes from June 23, 1972, so unusual that the president would make such a startling admission? Judge Sirica and Todd go to the jury room and load them up.

One of the tapes contains a conversation between Bob Haldeman, the president's chief of staff, and President Nixon. Haldeman refers to "the problem area," indicating it's a matter they've already discussed.

The FBI, Haldeman says, is not under control and is beginning to trace the money in the burglars' possession to the Committee to Re-elect the President. Haldeman discusses a plan to make "the problem" go away by asking the CIA to intervene with the FBI.

The president jumps in. "You call them in. Good. Good deal. Play it tough. That's the way they play it and that's the way we are going to play it."

"Okay, we'll do it," Haldeman replies.

"When you get these people in, say . . . the president just feels that . . . they should call the FBI in and say that 'we wish for the country, don't go any further into this case.' Period!"

Judge Sirica takes off his headphones. He looks to see if the jury room door is closed before speaking. "He's asking the CIA to stop the FBI investigation. I think this is a knockout punch for the president."

"It does sound bad," Todd says.

"This is what they will call the 'smoking gun.' Obstruction of justice," the judge says.

He thought the very first tapes were bad enough—demonstrating Nixon's familiarity with the cover-up. But this tape, days after the burglary, shows that the president was actively involved in scheming and hatching illicit plans from the very earliest days.

The grand jury was on target with its conspiracy charge, the judge notes. He stares into space, lost in thought, as Todd puts the tapes back in the vault.

With the courthouse mostly closed for the summer and still awaiting motions from the White House, Judge Sirica joins his family in Rehoboth Beach for a little ocean, sunshine, and exercise along the boardwalk.

Even without the actual tapes, the newly released transcripts send shock waves through Republican leaders who have stood up for the president.

The entire front page of the *Washington Post* on August 6 spills over with six stories and one photo about the tapes of June 23, 1972, and the president's statement. "President Admits Withholding Data; Tapes Show He Approved Cover-Up" reads the text streaming across the top of the page.

The article by Bob Woodward and Carl Bernstein reads: "President Nixon personally ordered a cover-up of the facts of Watergate within six days after the illegal entry into the Democrats' National Headquarters on June 17, 1972, according to three new transcripts of Mr. Nixon's conversations.

"The transcripts completely undermine the president's previous insistence that he was uninvolved in the cover-up. The transcripts demonstrate Mr. Nixon approved a plan to have the Central Intelligence Agency falsely claim that full FBI investigation into Watergate would expose covert operations of the agency."

Nine of the ten Republican members on the House Judiciary Committee who had voted against impeachment change their minds. A count in the full House of Representatives shows an overwhelming majority will vote for the articles of impeachment; a tally in the Senate indicates that almost all will vote for removing the president from office, a first in the nation's history.

A group of Republican leaders makes an appointment to meet with the president in the White House.

On August 8, a rainy and steamy day in the nation's capital, the White House press secretary announces that the president will deliver a televised statement to the nation from the Oval Office at 9 p.m.

On the dinnertime evening news, Walter Cronkite, the nation's preeminent broadcaster, leads with the breaking story. "President Nixon will reportedly announce his resignation tonight. And Vice President Ford will become the nation's thirty-eighth president tomorrow. That word comes unofficially from aides and associates of the two men, but not from the men themselves.

"Since Monday when President Nixon released a new tape, the smoking pistol of the Watergate evidence that tied it directly to him, events have been rushing toward one seemingly inevitable conclusion: removal from office. Mr. Nixon has chosen to take that step himself."

At 9 p.m., Judge Sirica switches on the TV at the beach house they're renting. Lucy sits by him on a couch while his two daughters sprawl on the floor.

President Nixon appears, sitting behind his wide wooden desk, blue drapes drawn behind him. Wearing a suit and a crisp white shirt with cuff links, he holds half a dozen sheets of paper in both hands in front of him.

"I have concluded that because of the Watergate matter, I might not have the support of the Congress that I would consider necessary to back the very difficult decisions and carry out the duties of this office in the way the interests of the nation would require.

"I have never been a quitter. To leave office before my term is completed is abhorrent to every instinct in my body. But as president, I must put the interests of America first. America needs a full-time president and a full-time Congress, particularly at this time with the problems we face at home and abroad.

"To continue to fight through the months ahead for my personal vindication would almost totally absorb the time and attention of both the president and the Congress in a period when our entire focus should be on the great issues of peace abroad and prosperity without inflation at home.

"Therefore, I shall resign the presidency effective at noon tomorrow. Vice President Ford will be sworn in as president at that hour."

There is nothing of regret or apology. Judge Sirica stares at the TV, as if he could will it to say more. He has a quiet moment of reflection: *After all that has happened, the soon-to-be ex-president seems unable to recognize the harm he has done to the nation.*

Chapter Eighteen

THE WORK OF THE COURT

The Watergate cover-up trial is still pending when the president resigns.

The public breathes a sigh of relief. But no one has reckoned with the fact that the president is named as a co-conspirator in the cover-up case. Now that he's out of office, he can be charged with a crime.

On September 8, exactly one month after President Nixon resigns, the new president, Gerald Ford, announces that he is giving Nixon "a full and absolute pardon for all offenses against the United States which he has committed or may have committed." Nixon has suffered enough, he says, and charges against him could destroy the "tranquility" of the nation.

Judge Sirica says nothing publicly, but he writes notes in a folder and sticks them in his desk drawer.

Richard Nixon should be—should have been—tried

in court like the other defendants. The Ford pardon is
wrong. No man is above the law!

Polls show that the majority of the people agree with him. In fact, only 38 percent approve of the pardon, and Ford's popularity drops dramatically.

On October 1, the cover-up case is finally on the court's calendar. Looking out from his high-backed chair, Judge Sirica sees a conglomeration of some of the most formidable attorneys in the country in front of the bar. On his left side, a team of exceptionally prepared lawyers from the special prosecutor's office. On his right, the defendants. There are five now. Charles Colson has decided to plead guilty, and his sentencing is being handled by another judge. Gordon Strachan's case is separated out because the Senate Watergate Committee had granted him immunity. This leaves some of the most powerful, or formerly powerful, defendants to face charges in a U.S. criminal court, ever. All but one—Nixon's right-hand man, Haldeman—are lawyers, and all have their own high-powered lawyers representing them.

One thing they share in common: They all seem to want to make objections to everything. Every minute, Judge Sirica is called upon to rule on one motion and then another. These lawyers seem to want to make sure that every phrase, word, and comma will be available for possible appeal.

It's mid-October before they can start taking testimony.

"What we are trying to get, members of the jury, is the truth of what happened," the judge tells the jurors. "You can sum up the case in one little word at the proper time—an objective finding by the jury of the truth, T-R-U-T-H."

"Objection!"

One lawyer objects, and then another, and another, varying

only in tonality and vocal range. The language should be stricken from the record, the lawyers say, because a trial is something quite different—a determination of whether or not the defendants are guilty beyond a reasonable doubt.

"Overruled," says Judge Sirica. "The court is interested in the truth. Now let's proceed."

The defense lawyers take two tacks. One is to place all of the blame on John Dean and Jeb Magruder, both of whom have already accepted guilty pleas. The other is to blame Richard Nixon, who is now pardoned and free from being tried.

Some of the lawyers want to call Nixon to testify, and Judge Sirica agrees. But before the scheduled date, doctors in California say that Nixon is ill, so ill, in fact, that he is entering the hospital, and unable to make the trip to D.C. Judge Sirica sends out a team of doctors to investigate; they agree that it would be harmful to Nixon's health to travel. At least, the judge thinks, the tapes will be introduced as evidence and the jurors will hear the ex-president in his own words.

John Dean is brought from his cell to testify—he'd been sentenced on his guilty plea by Judge Sirica in the fall. All in all, the prosecution presents thirty witnesses. The jurors listen to twenty hours of tapes through specially ordered headsets.

This time, the whole sordid affair spins out in the judge's courtroom. It is what Judge Sirica had suspected when the burglars came before him two years earlier, only worse. Hearing each detail, each planned, nefarious activity laid out day after day is shocking—from secret stashes of cash set aside for dirty tricks to surveillance, hush money for payoffs, attempted interference with investigators, and false testimony to frustrate the justice system.

The trial lasts for eleven weeks. On January 1, 1975,

two years and six-and-a-half months after the break-in at the Watergate complex, the jurors reach their verdict. Mitchell and Haldeman are guilty on five counts, Ehrlichman is guilty on four counts, Mardian is guilty on one count (later overturned because his lawyer became ill). Parkinson, who served at the Republican Committee for only a short period, is found not guilty.

A week later, Judge Sirica, mindful of John Dean's eight days on the stand, straightforward and unwavering, lets the former White House counsel out of prison for time served—a matter of a few months instead of the one- to four-year sentence originally handed down.

But Mitchell, Haldeman, and Ehrlichman must come back into court in late February for their sentencing hearings. Haldeman's lawyer argues that "whatever Bob Haldeman did, so did Richard Nixon; that Nixon has been freed of judicial punishment, yet Bob Haldeman has had to endure agony and punishment by the trial and conviction."

Judge Sirica turns away from the defense lawyer, an old friend from his days in the criminal defense bar decades earlier. His old friend surely knows that the judge is a Republican and campaigned at one point for Richard Nixon as the candidate on the vice-presidential ticket with Eisenhower. But does his old friend also understand that the judge believes that Nixon belongs in court, too? That Nixon and his underlings have betrayed public trust in the worst way possible?

Picking up a document on which he has notated the sentences, Judge Sirica tells the men that they will be serving a minimum of two-and-a-half years in prison to a maximum of eight years.

He doesn't have to read the newspaper the next day to know what it says. "Defense lawyers thought the sentences severe, but not surprising in light of Sirica's reputation for dealing out stiff terms. 'Maximum John,' says one."

But the judge wonders: *Did the cover-up defendants pay attention to what he told Gordon Liddy? The knowing and deliberate violation of laws deserves a greater condemnation than a simple careless or uncomprehending violation. The cases are a warning to all those down the road who may consider transgressing the law.*

The defendants can, of course, later apply for a sentence reduction. As he leaves the bench after sentencing, the judge vows to himself that at such a juncture he will ask a probation officer to visit each of the men in prison with a tape recorder, and to ask them what they think about their crimes and their responsibilities as high officials of the government.

He knows what he thinks: *No one, even the highest official in the land, is above the law.*

Epilogue

THE MEANING OF JUSTICE

In early 1979, Tom Marinelli asks Judge Sirica if he might drop by his home. Marinelli is the current president of the Lido Civic Club. He sits down with the judge in the living room.

"I'm going to get straight to the point, Your Honor," Marinelli says.

People still call him "Your Honor" or "Judge" even though he's now on retired senior status and handles cases only occasionally.

"Ya know me, Tom. I like it when people say what's on their minds," the judge replies.

"In 1974, Your Honor, you were named *Time Man of the Year*." Marinelli pulls the magazine clipping out of his sports jacket.

"Yes, yes. I recall."

"Says here—"

"I know what it says, Tom."

"I'd like to read it, Judge. 'Judge John J. Sirica: Standing Firm for the Primacy of Law. One judge, stubbornly and doggedly pursuing the truth in his courtroom regardless of its political implications, forced Watergate into the light of investigative day.' That's really something, Judge."

"Five years of my life—Watergate. Five years of stress!"

"The Lido Civic Club has never had such a luminary in our midst. I mean, we have a lot of good men—"

"Excellent men. Without the Lido Civic Club, I don't know how I would have ever gotten a foothold as a young man. And the scholarships—very important. We have to keep up the scholarship program."

"That's exactly what we were thinking, Your Honor. Now, several years back . . . 1974, I think, right after *Time Man of the Year*, we wanted to give you a testimonial dinner."

"No offense to Lido—I turned everyone down. Conflict of interest. Watergate cases were still going on. I explained to some of the Lido fellows back then."

"I've heard." Marinelli nods to show how closely he is listening.

"That was the year the tapes went up to the Supreme Court, and the president was ordered to deliver them. Then there was the 'smoking gun' tape, the House Judiciary impeachment vote, the president's resignation, the pardon . . . followed by the cover-up trial—and with all of the objections from all of the lawyers, I almost had a heart attack on the bench. What a sad situation to see John Mitchell, the former attorney general, in court like a common criminal—but those are the choices he made. Of course, there were appeals . . . endless appeals. Mitchell and Haldeman managed to put off their prison terms until 1977—more than two years after I sentenced them. Most of those men are out now—reduced sentences and all—but think how powerful they once were. Quite a lesson for the country."

"Indeed," Marinelli chimes in.

"Of course, the stress finally got to me. In '76. My heart. I was giving a speech, and boom—don't know what happened. I fell over. Luckily, some quick attention on the spot saved me. My youngest, Eileen, was only in eighth grade. I remember my son, Jack—he's the oldest, and then Patricia is in the middle— Jack wrote to my wife, 'He's been doing everything himself his whole life that it's hard for him to stop—even at seventy-three. For all the years of Watergate, I don't think he ever really took a vacation.' Of course not! How could I?"

"I hope that you're fully recovered now, Judge."

"Yes, yes. You may have heard—I'm a *retired* senior judge now. That means I only sit on the bench from time-to-time on an as-needed basis."

"Good, good. Because, Judge, we would like to have that testimonial dinner in your honor in the fall this year. It's our fiftieth anniversary." Marinelli holds out a letter to the judge. "We've named you the Lido Civic Club Man of the Year."

"Well, I thank you all. Very kind. But if I agree to do it, Tom, promise me that any proceeds will go to the scholarship fund."

"You have a deal, Your Honor."

When the time comes, the judge wishes his parents were alive to attend his Lido Civic Club dinner. His mother lived long enough to see him become a judge, but she had passed more than a dozen years before Watergate and the *Time* magazine honors and the other awards and commendations. He muses that he should suggest favorites from his mother's kitchen for the menu—spaghetti or lasagna and sausages with a hint of Naples, and cherries soaked in wine for dessert.

The ballroom menu that the Sheraton Park Hotel sends over before the event is a classic banquet: chicken cordon bleu, fresh spinach salad, bombe Grand Duc for dessert, with the added touch of Frascati and Ruffino wines.

"I expect I'll be too nervous to eat," Lucy says as she points the judge to the zipper on the back of her blue satin dress.

"You'll be fine," the judge says quietly.

"You won't be talking about me or the family, will you?" Lucy asks.

"Ya know me. Not in a specific way. Only to say thank you."

"It makes me uncomfortable when people stare in my direction."

"I'll talk about Coco instead." The judge looks around the corners of the room. "Think of what that little one experienced—five years of being awakened at three in the morning to the sound of Watergate."

"The anniversary committee says that Mario Segretti will sing the national anthem. The ladies tell me that Paolo Pansa Cedronio from the Italian Embassy will be there, too. There are more than 1,200 reservations."

"Friendly faces. Jack Dempsey sent me a note of regret. But we'll see our old Lido friends. Attorney General Benjamin Civiletti. Judges from the courthouse. Members of Congress. The mayor."

"My goodness. Can't you let me hear what you plan to say? I'd like to be prepared," Lucy says.

Judge Sirica closes the buttons on his tux and reaches for a handful of pages in a bureau drawer. He clears his throat.

"What I plan to say:

"I am the son of an immigrant father, Fred Sirica, who came to the United States from Italy as a child, and taught me reverence for America and integrity in my dealings with others. In the Lido Civic Club, an organization formed by the sons of Italian immigrants, I shared a sense of camaraderie and pride at a time when many of Italian descent, including my father, were derided and mocked. I was a young would-be boxer who somehow became a lawyer. The energy and guidance of the Lido Civic Club sustained me, guiding my path as a lawyer and judge. Lido helped Italians move into the mainstream of American society and, as a result, I became only the second person of Italian heritage chosen for the federal bench."

He takes a breath and glances over at Lucy.

"I learned some things along the way. Our country is blessed with a strong, independent legal system. The Constitution of the United States is a remarkable document. The founders created a government based upon the rule of law and not of men, placing no man, no matter how powerful or influential, above the reach of the law.

"Every man and woman, although he or she may not fully understand the complexities of our legal system, wants to be treated fairly and has a desire to see that justice prevails.

"There exists, in addition to a public justice, a private kind of justice. This type of justice is exercised in our dealings with our fellow Americans in the area of good conduct, morality, and character. It involves such things as fair play, equal opportunity, and person-to-person neighborly concern for the rights and freedoms of others.

"St. Thomas Aquinas once said, 'Justice is certain rectitude of mind whereby a man does what he ought to do in the circumstances confronting him.' What does this mean? That, at the end of the day, you must be able to look in the mirror and know that you've done the right thing.

"In law school and from legal mentors, I learned about the contours and ridges of the public kind of justice and that helped shape me as Judge John J. Sirica. These people helped me be clear and stand firm when the times called for it. In the Lido Civic Club and at home with my family—Lucy and our three children and our dog, Coco—the places where I will always be simply John or Johnny Sirica, or even Daddy—I came to cherish a private kind of justice. In times of difficulty that sense of duty and honor sustained me. For that, and for the many kindnesses of fellowship over the past fifty years, I thank you."

Lucy starts digging through a dresser drawer. "I can see that I'm going to need a handkerchief," she says.

"Ya know, I'm not dead yet," he says.

"Is there a title?" She stuffs the cloth hanky in her bag and snaps it closed.

Judge Sirica carefully folds the pages into the inner pocket of his tux.

"Yes," he says. "'No Person Above the Law.'"

About the Author

Cynthia Cooper is a playwright, journalist, and author. As a former practicing attorney, she often writes on topics of law and justice. Her plays have won several awards and have been produced in New York, Los Angeles, Chicago, Philadelphia, Washington D.C., Boston, Buffalo, Minneapolis, Reno, Montreal, Budapest, Jerusalem, and more, and have been published in sixteen volumes. She has authored or coauthored seven nonfiction books; one, *Mockery of Justice*, was made into a CBS-TV movie. She lives in New York City.

NOW AVAILABLE FROM THE MENTORIS PROJECT

America's Forgotten Founding Father
A Novel Based on the Life of Filippo Mazzei
by Rosanne Welch, PhD

A. P. Giannini—The People's Banker
by Francesca Valente

The Architect Who Changed Our World
A Novel Based on the Life of Andrea Palladio
by Pamela Winfrey

A Boxing Trainer's Journey
A Novel Based on the Life of Angelo Dundee
by Jonathan Brown

Breaking Barriers
A Novel Based on the Life of Laura Bassi
by Jule Selbo

Building Heaven's Ceiling
A Novel Based on the Life of Filippo Brunelleschi
by Joe Cline

Building Wealth
From Shoeshine Boy to Real Estate Magnate
by Robert Barbera

Building Wealth 101
How to Make Your Money Work for You
by Robert Barbera

Christopher Columbus: His Life and Discoveries
by Mario Di Giovanni

Dark Labyrinth
A Novel Based on the Life of Galileo Galilei
by Peter David Myers

Defying Danger
A Novel Based on the Life of Father Matteo Ricci
by Nicole Gregory

The Divine Proportions of Luca Pacioli
A Novel Based on the Life of Luca Pacioli
by W. A. W. Parker

Dreams of Discovery
A Novel Based on the Life of the Explorer John Cabot
by Jule Selbo

The Faithful
A Novel Based on the Life of Giuseppe Verdi
by Collin Mitchell

Fermi's Gifts
A Novel Based on the Life of Enrico Fermi
by Kate Fuglei

FUTURE TITLES FROM THE MENTORIS PROJECT

A Biography about Rita Levi-Montalcini
and
Novels Based on the Lives of:
Amerigo Vespucci
Andrea Doria
Antonin Scalia
Antonio Meucci
Buzzie Bavasi
Cesare Beccaria
Father Eusebio Francisco Kino
Federico Fellini
Frank Capra
Guido d'Arezzo
Harry Warren
Leonardo Fibonacci
Maria Gaetana Agnesi
Mario Andretti
Peter Rodino
Pietro Belluschi
Saint Augustine of Hippo
Saint Francis of Assisi
Vince Lombardi

For more information on these titles and
the Mentoris Project, please visit
www.mentorisproject.org

Made in the USA
Middletown, DE
05 February 2025